Sundays in August

ENGLISH TRANSLATIONS OF WORKS BY PATRICK MODIANO

From Yale University Press
After the Circus
Little Jewel
Paris Nocturne
Pedigree: A Memoir
Such Fine Boys
Sundays in August
Suspended Sentences: Three Novellas (Afterimage, Suspended Sentences, and Flowers of Ruin)

Also available or forthcoming
The Black Notebook
Catherine Certitude
Dora Bruder
Honeymoon
In the Café of Lost Youth
Lacombe Lucien
Missing Person
Out of the Dark
So You Don't Get Lost in the Neighborhood
The Occupation Trilogy (The Night Watch, Ring Roads, and La Place de l'Etoile)
A Trace of Malice
Villa Triste
Young Once

PRAISE FOR *SUSPENDED SENTENCES:*

"Vividly translated by Mark Polizzotti . . . [and] as good a place as any to enter the long, slow-moving river of Modiano's fiction."

ALAN RIDING, *New York Times Book Review*

"A timely glimpse at [Modiano's] fixations. . . . In Mark Polizzotti's spare and elegant translation, the writing conveys a sense of dreamy unease in which the real, the hypothesized, and the half-forgotten blend into a shimmering vagueness."

SAM SACKS, *Wall Street Journal*

"Mr. Modiano writes clear, languid, and urbane sentences in Mr. Polizzotti's agile translation. . . . These novellas have a mood. They cast a spell."

DWIGHT GARNER, *New York Times*

"Elegant . . . quietly unpretentious, approachable. . . . Though enigmatic and open-ended, Modiano's remembrances of things past and his probings of personal identity are presented with a surprisingly light touch. He is, all in all, quite an endearing Nobelist."

MICHAEL DIRDA, *Washington Post*

PRAISE FOR *PARIS NOCTURNE:*

"This novel provides a superb and—at 160 pages—accessible entry to [Modiano's] writings. . . . The narrator's search for Jacqueline propels the novel forward with the intensity of a noir. But Modiano is not writing mere pulp; the novel's true center is the past's pull, the way memories lay dormant for years only to explode 'like a time bomb.'"

Publishers Weekly

PRAISE FOR *AFTER THE CIRCUS:*

"[*After the Circus*] transposes Modiano's favorite themes into a taut, hard-boiled crime story. . . . Modiano is writing metaphysical mystery stories, in which the search for answers is never afforded an easy solution. The more of Modiano's work you read, the more familiar and inevitable his peculiar set of obsessions starts to feel—which is one sign of a major writer."

ADAM KIRSCH, *Daily Beast*

04470904

Sundays in August

PATRICK MODIANO

TRANSLATED FROM THE FRENCH BY DAMION SEARLS

YALE UNIVERSITY PRESS ■ NEW HAVEN & LONDON

A MARGELLOS
WORLD REPUBLIC OF LETTERS BOOK

The Margellos World Republic of Letters is dedicated to making literary works from around the globe available in English through translation. It brings to the English-speaking world the work of leading poets, novelists, essayists, philosophers, and playwrights from Europe, Latin America, Africa, Asia, and the Middle East to stimulate international discourse and creative exchange.

Yale University Press books may be purchased in quantity for educational, business, or promotional use. For information, please e-mail sales.press@yale.edu (U.S. office) or sales@yaleup.co.uk (U.K. office).

Set in Electra and Nobel types by Tseng Information Systems, Inc.
Printed in the United Kingdom by Hobbs the Printers Ltd, Totton.

Library of Congress Control Number: 2017940994
ISBN 978-0-300-22333-0 (paper : alk. paper)

A catalogue record for this book is available from the British Library.

This paper meets the requirements of ANSI/NISO z39.48-1992 (Permanence of Paper).

10 9 8 7 6 5 4 3 2 1

FOR JACQUES ROBERT
FOR MARC GRUNEBAUM

Sundays in August

Eventually our eyes met. It was in Nice, at the start of Boulevard Gambetta. He was standing on a kind of platform in front of a display of leather coats and jackets, and I had slipped to the front of the group of people listening to him tout his wares.

When he saw me, his salesman's patter faltered. He spoke more drily, as though wanting to establish a certain distance between himself and his listeners, to convey to me that this job he was doing on an outdoor platform was beneath him.

He hadn't changed much in seven years—his face seemed more flushed, that was all. It started to get dark and a gust of wind rushed down Boulevard Gambetta bearing the first drops of rain. A woman with curly blond hair was trying on a coat next to me. He leaned down from his platform toward her and gave her an encouraging look.

"It looks great on you."

His voice still had its metallic tone, a metal that had rusted a little over the years. The crowd was already dispersing, because of the rain, and the blonde took the coat off and placed it timidly on the edge of the display shelf.

"It's a real bargain, ma'am. American prices. You should . . ."

But without giving him time to finish, she turned quickly

away, hurrying off with the rest of the crowd. She looked like someone embarrassed to hear a stranger on the street making obscene suggestions.

He came down from his platform and walked over to me.

"What a nice surprise. I've got an eagle eye, I spotted you right away."

He seemed self-conscious, almost shy. I, on the other hand, felt calm and relaxed.

"It's funny seeing each other again here, isn't it?" I said.

"Yes."

He smiled. He had regained his confidence. A van stopped at the curb in front of us and a man in a red jacket got out.

"You can take it all down," he said, then he looked me straight in the eye. "Come have a drink?"

"If you want."

"I'm going to have a drink with him at the Forum," he said. "Come get me in half an hour."

The other man started loading the coats and jackets from the display stand into the van, while a steady stream of customers flowed past us out the doors of the large department store on the corner with Rue de la Buffa. A high-pitched sound announced closing time.

"Too bad . . . It's hardly raining anymore."

He was wearing a thin leather bag on a shoulder strap.

We crossed the boulevard and walked down the Promenade des Anglais. The café was nearby, next to the Forum Cinema. He picked a table at the bay window and dropped onto the bench.

"What's new?" he said. "You're here on the Riviera?"

I wanted to put him at ease. "It's funny," I said, "I saw you the other day on the Promenade des Anglais."

"You should have said hello."

His enormous silhouette, the long Promenade, that shoulder bag some men like to wear when they hit fifty, with jackets that are too tight, to try to look young . . .

"I've been working around here for a while. Trying to unload leather goods."

"How's business?"

"Not too bad. What about you?"

"I have a job around here too," I said. "Nothing interesting."

Out the window, the tall streetlamps on the Promenade were gradually coming on. First, a wavering violet glow that any breath of wind could put out like a candle. But it didn't go out. In an instant, the unsteady light turned white and hard.

"So, we're working in the same neck of the woods," he said. "I'm staying in Antibes. But I travel a lot . . ."

His bag opened the way a schoolboy's satchel does. He took out a pack of cigarettes.

"You haven't been back to Val-de-Marne, have you?" I asked.

"No. That's over."

There was an awkward moment between us.

"And you?" he asked. "Have you been back?"

"Never."

The mere thought of finding myself back on the banks of the Marne made me shudder. I looked out at the Promenade des Anglais, the darkening orange sky, the sea. Yes, I was really in Nice. It made me breathe a sigh of relief.

"I wouldn't go back there for anything in the world," I said.

"Me neither."

The waiter put the orange juice, brandy and water, and glasses on the table. I focused entirely on my every gesture, and he on his; it was as if we were trying to delay the moment of restarting our conversation for as long as possible. Finally it was he who broke the silence.

"I wanted to clear something up with you." And he looked at me through narrowed eyes. "Sylvia and I weren't actually married. My mother opposed the marriage . . ."

For a fraction of a second, I could see Madame Villecourt's shape before me, on the landing on the Marne.

"You remember my mother. She wasn't an easy woman. There were money issues between us, and she would have cut me off if I had married Sylvia."

"I don't believe it."

"Well, there it is."

I thought I was dreaming. Why had Sylvia lied to me? I remembered she even wore a ring.

"She wanted people to think we were married. It was a matter of pride for her. And I acted like a real coward . . . I should have married her."

I had to face facts: this man was nothing like the man I knew seven years ago. There was none of the arrogant rudeness that had made me hate him then. On the contrary, he was resigned now, quiet. His hands had changed. He no longer wore that thick chain bracelet.

"If I had married her, everything would have been different."

"You think so?"

He was obviously talking about someone other than Sylvia. Things meant something different to him in retrospect than they did to me.

"She never forgave me for being such a coward. She loved me. I'm the only man she loved."

His sad smile was as surprising as his leather shoulder bag. No, this wasn't the same man as the one from the Marne. Maybe he had forgotten whole stretches of the past, or had gradually convinced himself that certain events, with such serious consequences for us both, had never happened. I felt an irresistible desire to shake him.

"And your plan for the restaurant and swimming pool on the little island off Chennevières?"

I had raised my voice and leaned my face right up close to his. But the question didn't faze him; he just kept his same sad smile.

"I don't know what you mean . . . I used to look after my mother's horses, you remember. She had two trotters she entered in races in Vincennes."

He sounded so innocent that I couldn't argue.

"You saw that guy loading my coats into the van? He gambles

on horses. There can never be anything but misunderstandings between men and horses, if you ask me . . ."

Was he making fun of me? No—he had never had the least sense of humor. And the weary, serious expression on his face was only accentuated by the neon light.

"Things rarely work out between men and horses. I've tried to tell him not to bet on the races, he keeps doing it but he always loses money . . . Anyway, what about you? Are you still a photographer?"

He had pronounced the last word of his question in that metallic voice of his from seven years ago.

"I didn't really understand the photography book you were planning to do back then."

"I wanted to take pictures of the beaches along the rivers near Paris," I said.

"The beaches along the rivers? Is that why you were staying in La Varenne?"

"Yes."

"But there isn't really a beach there."

"No? There was Le Beach . . ."

"Well I guess you never had time to take your photographs?"

"Yes I did. I can show you some of them if you want . . ."

Our conversation had become relaxed. It was strange to be expressing ourselves this way—implicitly, with insinuations.

"In any case, I certainly learned a lot. It was a very educational time for me."

He didn't react to my comment at all, even though I had

made it quite aggressively. I insisted: "You too, I imagine. You must have bad memories of all that?"

But I immediately felt bad for trying to provoke him. It slid right off him anyway, and he gave me a sad smile.

"I don't remember anything anymore," he said. He glanced at his watch. "He'll be here to get me soon . . . Too bad, I would have enjoyed sitting here with you a while. But I hope we'll see each other again?"

"You really want to see me again?"

I felt dizzy. At least if he were the same man as he was seven years ago, that would have been less disconcerting.

"Yes. I'd like it very much. We could meet up now and then to talk about Sylvia."

"Do you really think there's any point?"

How could I talk to him about Sylvia? I wasn't even sure whether, after seven years, he was confusing her with someone else. He remembered that I had been a photographer, but there are always some scraps of the past that survive in old men who've lost their memory: the taste of a childhood birthday cake, the words of a lullaby once sung to them . . .

"Don't you want to talk about her? Get it through your head . . ."

He gave the table a blow with his fist, and I was waiting to hear the threats and blackmail he used to come out with — diluted by time, of course, like the things doddering war criminals say in court when they're captured forty years after their misdeeds.

"Get it through your head that nothing would have happened if she and I had been married. Nothing. She loved me. The only thing she wanted was for me to show her I loved her too. And I couldn't . . ."

Seeing him sitting there in front of me, listening to these words of a repentant sinner, I wondered if I hadn't been unfair to him after all. He was rambling, but he had made progress. Back then, he would never have been able to pursue a chain of reasoning like this.

"I think you're wrong," I said. "But it doesn't matter. Your intentions are good in any case."

"I am absolutely not wrong." And he drunkenly pounded his fist on the table again. I was afraid he might turn back into his brutal and nasty old self. Luckily, just then, the man from the delivery van walked into the café and put a hand on his shoulder. He turned around and stared at him as though he didn't recognize him.

"Yes. Coming."

We stood up and I walked them back to the van, which was now parked in front of the Forum Cinema. He slid open the back door, revealing a row of leather coats on hangers.

"Help yourself."

I didn't move. He looked through them one by one, taking down hangers one at a time and then putting them back on the rods.

"This one should be your size."

He handed me the coat with the hanger still in it.

"I don't need a new coat," I said.

"Please, go ahead, I want you to have it."

The other man was sitting on the van's fender, waiting.

"Try it on."

I took the coat and put it on in front of him. He looked at me with the sharp eye of a tailor during a fitting.

"It's not too tight at the shoulders, is it?"

"No, but I'm telling you I don't need a coat."

"Take it, as a favor to me. I insist."

He buttoned it himself. I stood stiff as a wooden mannequin.

"It fits you well. The thing about me is I have a lot in large sizes . . ."

I took it so that I could be free of him faster. I didn't want to keep talking. I was in a hurry to see him leave.

"If there's anything wrong with it, come exchange it for another one. I'll be at my stand tomorrow afternoon. Boulevard Gambetta . . . Anyway, I'll give you my address."

He reached into an inside jacket pocket and handed me a business card.

"Here—my address and phone number in Antibes. I'm counting on you . . ."

He opened the van's side door, climbed in, and sat on a bench. The other man took his seat behind the wheel. He rolled down the window and leaned out.

"I know you don't like me," he said. "But I'm ready to make

amends. I've changed . . . I realize now what I did wrong, especially to Sylvia. I'm the only man she really loved . . . We'll talk more about Sylvia next time, right?"

He looked me up and down, head to toe.

"That coat looks great on you."

Then he rolled up the window, keeping his eye on me. Suddenly, just when the van started moving, his face froze in amazement: I hadn't been able to keep from flipping him off—a gesture incomprehensible from someone as reserved as I was.

People were going into the Forum Cinema for the nine o'clock showing. I was tempted to go too and sit on a red velvet seat in the old auditorium. But I wanted to get rid of that coat, which pinched my shoulders and made it hard for me to breathe. In my hurry to get it off, I tore off a button. I folded the coat and put it on a bench on the Promenade, then walked away feeling like I had left behind something compromising.

Was it the dilapidated façade of the Forum Cinema? Or Villecourt's reappearance? Whatever the reason, I found myself thinking back to what his mother had told me about the mysterious murder of the actor Raymond Aimos on a barricade in the Gare du Nord area during the liberation of Paris. Aimos had known too much, had heard too many conversations, rubbed shoulders with too many dubious characters in the hotels of

Chennevières, Champigny, La Varenne. And the names of all those people Madame Villecourt had told me about made me think of the slimy water of the Marne.

I looked at his card:

Frédéric Villecourt, Sales

Back then, his name would have been embossed in black. Today it was printed in orange, like the words of a simple brochure, and to anyone who knew the Frédéric Villecourt from the Marne the modest job title, "Sales," showed that a few years had been enough to strip him of his pretentions. He had written his address on the card in blue ink: 5 Avenue Bosquet, Antibes. Tel.: 50.22.83.

I walked down Boulevard Victor-Hugo, having decided to go back home on foot. No, I should never have tried to talk to him.

The first time, on the Promenade des Anglais, when I saw him walking by with his heavy gait and that ridiculous little leather shoulder bag, I did not feel the least desire to talk to him. It was a Sunday, in the gentle autumn sun, and I was sitting at an outdoor table at the Queenie. There he was, stopping to light a cigarette. He stayed where he was behind the stream of traffic for another moment. Had he crossed at the light he would have found himself just where I was on the sidewalk. Then he could have easily spotted me. Or else he might have stayed there unmoving, until night fell, and his silhouette black as India ink would stand out against the sea, before my eyes, forever.

He kept walking, toward the Ruhl casino and Jardin Albert I, leather bag on his shoulder. All around me men and women, stiff as mummies, drank their tea in silence, eyes fixed on the Promenade des Anglais. Maybe they, too, were on the lookout for silhouettes from their past amid this crowd passing before their eyes.

To get back to where I was living, I had to walk through what used to be the dining hall of the old Hotel Majestic, at the bend in Boulevard de Cimiez. Now it was just a large room available for meetings or conventions. All the way in back, in the semidarkness, a choir was singing hymns in English. The sign at the foot of the staircase said, in English: "Today: *The Holy Nest*." I could still hear their high-pitched voices when I closed the door to my room on the third floor. Christmas carols, apparently. It was the season. My furnished room, an old hotel room with a bathroom, was cold. The room number was still on a copper plate inside the wardrobe: 252.

I turned on the small electric heater, but it gave off so little warmth that I eventually unplugged it. I stretched out on the bed without taking off my shoes.

The Majestic building has three- and four-room apartments, formerly the hotel's suites or else single rooms connected to one another during the renovations. I always prefer living in a single room. It's less sad. You can keep the illusion that you're staying in a hotel. The bed is still the one from Room 252. The night table too. I wonder if the dark wood bureau, fake Louis XVI, was part of the Majestic's furniture. The carpeting hadn't existed during the time of Room 252: gray-beige wall-to-wall, worn in places. The tub and sink were new too.

I did not feel like eating. I turned off the light, closed my eyes, and let the distant voices of the English choir sing me to sleep. I was still stretched out on the bed, in the dark, when the phone rang.

"Hello. It's Villecourt."

His voice was very soft, almost a whisper.

"Am I bothering you? I found your number in the phone book."

I didn't say anything. He asked me again: "Am I bothering you?"

"Not at all."

"I just wanted things between us to be clear. When we said goodbye I got the impression you were angry at me."

"I wasn't angry at you."

"But that gesture you made . . ."

"I was only joking."

"Joking? You have a strange sense of humor."

"Well," I said, "that's just the way I am."

"It seemed very hostile . . . Is there something you're mad at me about?"

"No."

"I didn't approach you, you're the one who came looking for me, Henri. You were standing there waiting for me at the Boulevard Gambetta display."

"My name's not Henri."

"Sorry. I was mixing you up with someone else, the guy who always gave tips on the races. I don't know what Sylvia saw in him . . ."

"I don't want to talk to you about Sylvia."

It was truly painful having this conversation over the phone in the dark. The voices of the English singers still reached me from the hall, reassuring me that I wasn't completely alone.

"Why not?"

"Because we're not talking about the same person."

I hung up. The phone rang again almost immediately.

"Hanging up on someone is not very nice, but you can't get rid of me just like that."

He tried to sound ironic.

"I'm tired," I said.

"Me too. But that's no reason not to talk. We are the only people left who know certain things . . ."

"I thought you'd forgotten everything."

There was silence.

"Not really . . . That bothers you, doesn't it?"

"No."

"Get it through your head that I was the person who knew Sylvia the best. It was me she loved. I'm not trying to avoid responsibility for what happened, see?"

I hung up. Several minutes passed before the phone rang again.

"Sylvia and I shared a very strong bond. Nothing else mattered to her."

He talked as though he found it perfectly natural to have just been hung up on, twice. "I'd like to talk to you about all of that, whether you want to or not. I'll keep calling until you give in."

"I'll disconnect the phone."

"Then I'll wait for you outside your building. You can't give me the slip that easily. After all, it's you who came looking for me."

I hung up again, and again the phone rang.

"I haven't forgotten certain things . . . I can still cause you lots of problems. I want to have a serious talk with you about Sylvia."

"You forget that I can cause serious problems for you too," I said.

This time, after hanging up, I dialed my own number and then shoved the receiver under the pillow so that I couldn't hear the busy signal.

I got up and went over to press my forehead against the window, without turning on the light. The Boulevard de Cimiez down below was deserted. A car drove by every so often and, every time, I wondered if it was going to stop. The sound of a door. He would step out, raise his head toward the façade of the Majestic, looking to see which floor still had a light on. He would step into the phone booth at the bend in the street. Would I leave the receiver off the hook? Or would I answer? The best thing to do would be to wait for it to ring and then pick up and hold the receiver to my ear without saying a word. He would repeat: "Hello? Are you there? Hello, are you there? I'm right near your apartment. Answer me, answer me . . ." To this more and more uneasy, more and more plaintive voice I would offer only silence. Yes. I'd enjoy giving him the same feeling of empty space that I feel myself.

The choir had died down a long time ago, and I stayed at my post by the window. I was waiting for a shape to appear, down below, silhouetted against the white light of the boulevard, the way it had been the other Sunday on the Promenade des Anglais.

■

Late the next morning I went down to the garage, which you reach by going down a cement staircase from the ground floor. You have to go down a hall at the back of the dining room, open a door, and turn on a light on a timer.

It's a vast space below the Majestic, which must already have been a parking lot when the Majestic was a hotel.

No one there. The three employees were off for lunch. In truth, there was less and less work to do. Someone rang the bell at the service station attached to the garage. A Mercedes was waiting there, and the driver asked me to fill it up. He gave me a big tip.

Then I headed for my office inside the garage. A room with a tile floor, light-green walls, and glass dividers. Someone had left an envelope with my name on it on the white wooden table. I opened it and read:

Don't worry. You won't hear from me again.

From Sylvia either. —Villecourt

To satisfy my conscience, I took his card out of my pocket and called his Antibes number. No answer. I tidied up my office, where old invoices and files had been piling up for several months. I sorted them and put them away in the metal cabinet. Soon there was nothing left to do. The building manager, who had gotten me this job running the garage, had recently warned me that they were about to turn it into a basic parking lot.

I looked through the glass pane: an American car was waiting there, roof down, with a flat tire. When the others got back I would have to check and make sure they hadn't forgotten about it. But would they come back? They too had been told that the garage was about to be closed, and they had probably found another job somewhere else. I was the only one who hadn't taken any precautions.

Later, in the afternoon, I tried calling Villecourt's Antibes number again. No answer. Only one of the three garage workers had come back, and he fixed the flat tire. I told him that I'd be out for an hour or two and asked him to look after the service station.

It was sunny on Boulevard Dubouchage, with a carpet of dead leaves on the sidewalk. While I walked I thought about my future. I would get severance when the garage closed and I could live for a while on that. I would keep my room at the Majestic—the rent was almost nothing. I might be able to convince Boistel, the building manager, to let me not pay rent at all, in return for my services. Yes, I would stay on the Riviera forever. What was the point of a new horizon? I could take up my old job as a photographer and stand with my Polaroid on the Promenade des Anglais, where the tourists walk by. What I had thought when I saw Villecourt's business card applied to me too: a few years was enough to bring an end to my pretentions.

Without realizing it, I had reached the Jardin d'Alsace-Lorraine. I turned left onto Boulevard Gambetta and felt a slight clenching of the heart. I wondered if I would find Villecourt back at his display stand. This time, I would watch him from afar so that he wouldn't notice me, and leave before too long. It would be a relief to watch this guy peddling jackets, who was no longer the old Villecourt, and who had never played any role in my life. Never. A harmless hawker like you find everywhere on the streets of Nice as Christmas approaches. Nothing more.

I made out a shape moving behind the display stand. As I crossed Rue de la Buffa, I saw that it wasn't Villecourt but a tall blond with a horsey face and a plaid jacket. I slipped to the front, just like the first time. He was not using the platform, or the microphone; he spoke his patter in a loud voice and reeled off the various goods he had on offer: beaver fur, lambskin, rabbit, skunk, plain or fur-lined leather boots . . . The display had many more items on it than yesterday, and this blond had attracted a bigger crowd than Villecourt. Much less leather. Lots of fur. Maybe Villecourt wasn't thought worthy of selling fur.

He was offering the beaver-fur and short-fitted lambskin jackets at twenty percent off. Lambskin? There were all colors:

black, chocolate brown, navy blue, metallic olive green, fuchsia, lilac . . . and a bag of roasted chestnuts with every purchase. He spoke faster and faster until I started to get dizzy. Eventually I took a seat at the outdoor café next to the stand and waited almost an hour until the crowds dispersed. It had gotten dark a long time ago.

He was alone, behind the display stand, and I went over to him.

"It's closed," he said. "But if you want something, I have jackets at very good prices. Thirty percent off. Long soft-wool jackets . . . taffeta lining . . . sizes 38 to 46 . . . I'll give it to you for half price . . ."

If I hadn't interrupted him he would have never stopped. His momentum just kept him going.

"Do you know Frédéric Villecourt?" I asked him.

"No."

He started stacking up his furs and jackets.

"But he was here yesterday, in your place."

"We have lots of France Leather salesmen on the Riviera, you know."

The van stopped next to the display stand, and the same driver got out and slid the door open.

"Hello," I said. "We met last night, with a friend of mine."

He looked at me, brow furrowed, and seemed not to remember a thing.

"You came to get us at the Forum café."

"Oh, right."

"Load this all fast for me," the tall horse-faced blond said.

The driver picked up the coats and jackets, one after the other, and put them on hangers before hanging them in the van.

"You don't know where he is?"

"Maybe he doesn't work for France Leather anymore." He said this drily, as though Villecourt had committed a very grave error in forgoing the privilege of working for France Leather.

"I thought he had a permanent job."

The tall blond with the horsey face, sitting on the edge of the display stand, was making notes in a little notebook. The day's sales?

I took Villecourt's card out of my pocket.

"You must have taken him home last night. 5 Avenue Bosquet, in Antibes."

The driver went on arranging the coats and jackets in the van, not bothering even to glance at me.

"That's a hotel," he told me. "Where the France Leather salesmen stay. Then they're told whether they're needed in Cannes or in Nice."

I handed him a lambskin coat, then a leather jacket, then a pair of fur-lined boots. If I helped him load the van, maybe he would deign to give me some more information about Villecourt.

"What makes you think I have time to get to know them all? It's a revolving door, a dozen new guys every week. They're here two or three days then they leave again. Others come and replace them . . . There's no downtime with France Leather. We have stands everywhere in the area, not just in Cannes or Nice. In Grasse, in Draguignan . . ."

"So there's no chance of finding him in Antibes?"

"Not a chance. I'm sure someone else is in his room by now. Maybe Mister . . ." And he gestured to the tall horse-faced blond, still writing in his notebook.

"There's no way to find out where he is?"

"There are two possibilities. Either he doesn't work for France Leather anymore, they fired him because he wasn't a good salesman . . ."

He had finished hanging his coats and jackets in the van and was wiping his brow with the end of his scarf.

" . . . Or they sent him somewhere else. But if you ask the main office, they won't tell you anything. Professional secrets. You're not a member of the family, are you?"

"No."

Now his tone was gentler. The tall horse-faced blond came over to us.

"All packed up?"

"Yes."

"So let's go."

He got into the front of the van, while the other man slid the back door shut and checked to make sure it was locked. Then he got in on his side and leaned out the open window to look at me.

"Sometimes France Leather sends them abroad. There are warehouses in Belgium. If that happened, if they sent him to Belgium . . ."

He shrugged his shoulders and started the van. I watched it turn onto the Promenade des Anglais and disappear.

■

It was warm out. I walked to the Jardin d'Alsace-Lorraine and sat on a bench behind the swings and the sandbox. I like it there, with the umbrella pines and the buildings silhouetted so sharply against the sky. I used to come sit here with Sylvia in the afternoon sometimes. We were safe, among all the mothers watching their children. No one would come looking for us here in the park, and the people here paid no attention to us. After all, we might have had children here too, going down the slide, building a sand castle . . .

In Belgium. If that happened, if they sent him to Belgium . . . I pictured Villecourt at night, in the rain, selling key rings and old pornographic photographs on the street in the area around the Gare du Midi in Brussels. A mere shadow of himself. The message he'd left for me that morning in the garage had come as no surprise: "You won't hear from me again." I had had a premonition of it. The surprising thing was that he had written to me at all, this message that constituted physical proof that he was still alive. When he was standing behind his display stand last night, it had taken me some time to recognize him, to convince myself that it was really him. I had planted myself in the front of the group of onlookers and stared right at him, as though trying to remind him of himself. And he, under this insistent stare, was forced to turn back into the old Villecourt. He had played that role again for a few hours, had called me on the phone, but his heart wasn't in it. Now, in Brussels, he walked back down Boulevard Anspach to the Gare du Nord and took a train at random. He found himself in a smoky compartment, filled with men travelling on business, playing cards. And the train departed for an unknown destination . . .

I too had thought about Brussels as a place to run away to, with Sylvia, but we had decided to stay in France. We needed a big city where we would pass unnoticed. There were half a million people in Nice, among whom we could disappear. It was not just any city. And then, too, the Mediterranean . . .

In the building on the corner between the little park and Boulevard Victor-Hugo, where Madame Efflatoun Bey used to live, there was a light on in a fourth-floor window. Was she still alive? I felt I should ring her doorbell or ask the concierge. I stared at the window filled with yellow light. Back when we first arrived in the city, Madame Efflatoun Bey had already lived a long life and I wondered if she had any vague memories of it. She was a friendly ghost among the thousands of other ghosts populating Nice. Sometimes, in the afternoon, she would come and sit on a bench next to us in the Jardin d'Alsace-Lorraine.

Ghosts never die. Their windows are always lit, like the windows in all the ochre and white buildings around me, their façades half hidden by the umbrella pines on the square. I stood up. I walked down Boulevard Victor-Hugo, involuntarily counting the plane trees.

At first, when Sylvia joined me in Nice, I saw things differently than I do this evening. Nice was not this familiar city where I walk back to the Majestic's hall and my room and my useless space heater. Luckily, winters are mild on the Riviera and I don't mind sleeping in a coat. It's spring that I'm afraid of. It comes back like a tidal wave every time, and every time I ask myself if it's going to knock me overboard.

I thought that my life was taking a new course, that all I needed to do was stay in Nice for a while to erase everything that had come before. We would end up no longer feeling the weight that was pressing down on us. That evening, I walked with a step much quicker than today. I passed a hair salon on Rue Gounod. Its pink neon still glows—I couldn't keep from checking before continuing my walk.

I was not yet a ghost myself, like I am tonight. I told myself that we would forget everything, that everything would start over in this unknown city. Start over. That's the phrase I kept repeating as I walked down Rue Gounod, with more and more of a skip in my step.

"Straight ahead," a passerby said when I asked the way to the station. Straight ahead. I had faith in the future. The streets were new to me. It didn't matter if I took a somewhat roundabout path. Sylvia's train wasn't due to arrive in Nice until ten-thirty that night.

■

Her luggage was a large garnet-colored leather bag and, around her neck, the Southern Cross. I felt suddenly nervous, seeing her walking toward me. I had left her in a hotel in Annecy a week before, to go to Nice alone and make sure we would be able to stay.

The Southern Cross sparkled on her black sweater under her open coat. Our eyes met and she smiled and flipped up her collar. It was reckless to wear the jewel so ostentatiously. What if she had found herself sitting across from a diamond dealer in the train and he had noticed? But this crazy thought eventually made me smile too. I took her bag.

"There wasn't a diamond dealer in your compartment, was there?"

I stared hard at the few travelers who had just gotten off the train in Nice, streaming all around us on the platform.

■

In the taxi I was briefly worried. Maybe she wouldn't like the place I had chosen, or how the apartment looked. But it was better for us to live somewhere like that than in a hotel where the employees at reception might be able to identify us.

The taxi followed the same path I am walking today, in reverse: Boulevard Victor-Hugo, Jardin d'Alsace-Lorraine. It was the same time of the year, late November, and the plane trees

had lost their leaves, just like tonight. She had taken the Southern Cross off from around her neck and I felt the chain and the
diamond in the palm of my hand.

"Here, take it. Otherwise I'll lose it."

I carefully slipped the Southern Cross into the inside pocket
of my jacket.

"You realize that if there'd been a diamond dealer sitting in
your compartment . . . ?"

She leaned her head on my shoulder. The taxi had stopped at
Rue Gounod to let the cars coming from the left pass. At the start
of the street, the hair salon's façade glowed neon pink.

"If there had been a diamond dealer, he would have thought
it was from Burma."

She had whispered this sentence in my ear so that the driver
wouldn't hear it, in the accent Villecourt had called "suburban-
ite" back when he was trying to seem distinguished—the voice I
loved because it was that of childhood.

"Yes, but what if he'd asked you if he could take a closer look,
with a magnifying glass?"

"I would have said it was a family jewel."

The taxi stopped at Rue Caffarelli, in front of the Sainte-
Anne, furnished rooms to let. We stood frozen for a moment on
the sidewalk, the two of us. I was holding her bag.

"The hotel's in the back," I said.

I was afraid she would be disappointed. But she took my arm,
I pushed open the gate that swung back in a rustle of leaves, and

we walked down the dark path to the pavilion lit by a bulb above the porch.

We walked past the porch. In the main room, where the owner had seen me to rent me the room for a month, the chandelier was on.

We went around the pavilion without anyone noticing us. I opened the back door and we went up the service stairs. The room was on the second floor, at the end of a hallway.

She sat down on the old leather armchair. She didn't take her coat off. She looked around, as if trying to get used to the décor. The two windows looking out on the pavilion's lawn were covered with black curtains. There was rose-patterned wallpaper except on the back wall—a light wood, suggesting a mountain chalet. There was no other furniture besides the leather chair and the rather large bed with brass bedposts.

I sat on the edge of the bed and waited for her to say something.

"Anyway, no one will come looking for us here."

"Definitely not," I said.

I tried to lay out for her the advantages of the place, partly to convince myself: I had paid a month in advance, there was a separate entrance, we would keep the key ourselves, the owner lived on the ground floor, she would leave us alone . . .

But she didn't seem to be listening to me. She was looking at the ceiling fixture as it cast a weak light over us, then the parquet floor, then the black curtains.

With her coat on, she looked like she was about to leave the room at any moment, and I was afraid of being left all alone on the bed. She stayed there without moving, her hands flat on the chair's armrests. A discouraged look passed over her face, the same discouragement I was feeling myself.

But she only had to look at me for it all to change. Maybe she could tell that we were feeling the same things at the same time. She smiled at me and softly said, as though afraid that someone might be listening at the door: "There's nothing to worry about."

The music and an announcer's deep voice coming from a speaker downstairs in the pavilion suddenly stopped. Someone had turned off the TV or radio. We were lying outstretched in bed. I had pulled back the curtains, and a feeble light from the two windows crossed the darkness of the room. I saw the side of her face. Her two arms reached up behind her head, hands gripping the bars of the bedframe, and the Southern Cross was at her neck. She liked wearing it while she slept—that way no one could steal it.

"Do you smell that strange smell?" she asked.

"Yes."

The first time I'd been in that room, the smell of mold had almost suffocated me. I had opened both windows to air out the room, but it hadn't helped. The odor had seeped into the walls, the leather chair, the wool bedspread.

I curled up to her and soon her perfume was stronger than the smell in the room, a heavy perfume I can't forget, something soft and shadowy, like the bonds that connect us to another person.

Tonight, in the one-time dining hall of the Hotel Majestic, is the weekly meeting of the Distant Lands Club. Instead of going up to my room, I could take a seat on one of the wooden benches—the same benches as outside in the parks—and listen to the talk along with a hundred other people gathered there, each with a white circle inscribed "D. L." in blue letters on the back of their coat. But there's no space free for me, and I slip past them to the stairs, brushing against the wall.

My room today is like the room in the Sainte-Anne Pension on Rue Caffarelli. The same smell fills the air in winter, from the humidity and the old wood and the leather furniture. Places rub off on you over time, but back on Rue Caffarelli, with Sylvia, I didn't think that way. Today, I often feel like I'm rotting away on the spot. And I'm right. The feeling goes away after a while and all that's left is a calm, detached sense of lightness. Nothing matters anymore. In the Rue Caffarelli days, I was discouraged sometimes but the future seemed bright. We would eventually get out of this dicey situation we were in. Soon, very soon, we would leave and go somewhere far away, abroad. I was fooling myself. I didn't know yet that this city was a morass, that I was getting stuck in it, little by little. And that the only path I would follow down through the years would be the one leading from Rue Caffarelli to Boulevard de Cimiez, where I live now.

The day after Sylvia arrived was a Sunday. We went to the Promenade des Anglais and sat at an outdoor table, in the late afternoon—the same one where, the other day, I saw Villecourt walk by, with his leather shoulder bag. He had finally joined the shadows passing before us, back-lit, these men and women like Sylvia and me, as old as we were . . . I get scared when I shut the door of my room. I wonder whether, from this point on, I am one of them. That evening, they were slowly sipping their tea at the tables next to ours. Sylvia and I watched them and all the others continuing to walk past us down the Promenade des Anglais. The end of a winter Sunday. And I know that we were thinking the same thing: that we had to find someone, among all those people ambling at the same time along the Riviera, to whom we could sell the Southern Cross.

■

It rained for several days in a row. I went to the newspaper stand at the edge of the Jardin d'Alsace-Lorraine and came back through the rain to the Sainte-Anne Pension. The owner was feeding her birds, dressed in an old raincoat and a scarf on her head tied under her chin to protect her from the rain. She was an elegant woman, around sixty, who spoke with a Parisian accent. She waved me over and said good morning, then continued to open her cages one by one, give the birds seeds, then close the cages.

Her too—what accidents of chance had made her wash up in Nice?

In the morning, when we woke up and heard the raindrops pounding on the tin roof of the little shed in the garden, we knew that it would be like that all day. We often stayed in bed until the end of the afternoon. It was better to wait until nighttime before going out. During the day, the rain on the Promenade des Anglais, on the pale buildings and the palm trees, made our hearts sink. It soaked the walls, and before long the pastry-shop colors and ridiculous décor were completely sodden. Nightfall wiped out this desolation, with the streetlamps and the neon.

The first time I had the feeling of being caught in a trap in this city, it was in the rain, on Rue Caffarelli, when I had gone out for newspapers. But when I got back to the room, my confidence returned. Sylvia was reading a mystery, her chest leaning against the bars of the bedframe and head hanging forward. As long as she was with me, I had nothing to fear. She was wearing a tight light-gray turtleneck that made her look even thinner and contrasted beautifully with her black hair and shining blue eyes.

"There's nothing in the newspapers?" she asked.

I flipped through them, sitting on the foot of the bed.

"No. Nothing."

Everything eventually blurs together. The images of the past blend into a light, transparent haze that thins out, swells up, and takes on the shape of an iridescent balloon about to burst. I wake up with a jolt, heart pounding. The silence only makes me more anxious. I can't hear the "Distant Lands" lecturer anymore, whose amplified monotone had reverberated all the way to my room. That voice, and the soundtrack to the documentary that followed—about the Pacific, no doubt, given the wails of the Hawaiian guitars—had lulled me to sleep.

I don't know anymore whether we met the Neals before or after Villecourt arrived in Nice. I have searched my memory, looking for points of reference, but am unable to sort out the two events. Anyway, there's no such thing as "events." Ever. It's a false term, suggesting something definitive, spectacular, brutal. In fact it all happened gently, imperceptibly, like the slow weaving of a design into a carpet, like the strolling people passing before our eyes on the sidewalk of the Promenade des Anglais.

At around six o'clock, we were sitting in the glassed-in terrace of the Queenie. Violet light flickered in the streetlamps. It was night. We were waiting, without quite knowing for what. We were like the hundreds and hundreds of people who, over the years, had also sat at the same table on the Promenade: refugees in the Free Zone, exiles, Englishmen, Russians, gigolos, Corsican croupiers from the Palais de la Méditerranée. Some of them hadn't budged in forty years and were drinking their tea at the tables next to ours with little halting gestures. And the pianist? How long had he been scattering his handfuls of notes in the back of the room from five to eight o'clock? I was curious enough to ask him. Since forever, he said. An evasive answer, like that of someone who has known an incriminating secret for too long and only wanted to conceal it. In other words, someone like Sylvia and me. And every time he saw us come in, he gave us a sign of recognition: a friendly nod or a few chords played on the piano with special emphasis.

That night, we stayed at our table later than usual. The other customers had slowly left the room, leaving no one there except the pianist and us. It was a moment of emptiness, before the first customers arrived for dinner. The waiters had set the tables in the restaurant part of the café. And we didn't know what to do that night. Go back to our room at the Sainte-Anne Pension? See a movie at the Forum Cinema? Or simply wait?

They sat down at a table near ours, side by side, facing us. He looked a bit disheveled in his suede jacket, face haggard as though he had just come back from a long trip or hadn't slept for twenty-four hours. She, on the other hand, was dressed up: her hair and makeup made it look like she was off to a party. She wore a fur coat that must have been sable.

It happened in the most natural, ordinary way. I think Neal came over to ask me for a light after a while. There was no one in the room except us and them, and they had realized it was closing time.

"Really, not even a drink?" Neal said with a smile. "We're completely on our own?"

A waiter headed listlessly over toward their table. I remember that Neal ordered a double espresso, which seemed to confirm my idea that he hadn't slept in a long time. In the back, the pianist was pressing the same keys over and over, doubtless to check that his instrument was in tune. No customers had come in for dinner. The waiters stood stock still in the room, waiting. And those notes from the piano, always the same ones . . . It was raining on the Promenade des Anglais.

"Great atmosphere they've got here," Neal remarked.

She smoked in silence, next to him. She smiled at us. There was a scrap of conversation between Neal and us:

"Do you live in Nice?"

"Yes, what about you?"

"Us too. Are you here on vacation?"

"It's not much fun when it rains in Nice."

"Maybe he could play something else," Neal said. "He's giving me a headache."

He stood up, walked into the room, and went over to the pianist. The woman was still smiling at us. As Neal came back, we heard the opening bars of "Strangers in the Night."

"Is this all right with you?" he asked us.

The waiter had brought the beverages and Neal invited us to have a round. Sylvia and I found ourselves at their table. The word "meet" doesn't apply, any more than "event." We didn't meet the Neals. They slipped into our net. If it hadn't been the Neals, that night, it would have been someone else, the next day or the day after that. For days and days Sylvia and I had been waiting, motionless in places people were moving through: hotel bars and lobbies, café tables along the Promenade des Anglais. It seems to me now that we were weaving a gigantic, invisible spiderweb and waiting for someone to find their way into it.

They both had faint foreign accents. Eventually I asked: "Are you English?"

"I'm American," Neal said. "My wife is English."

"I was raised on the Riviera," she corrected him. "I'm not entirely English."

"And I'm not entirely American," Neal said. "I've lived in Nice for a long time."

They forgot we were there, and then, the next moment, they spoke to us in a warm, friendly way. His mix of distraction and euphoria was due to exhaustion and jet lag: yesterday he had been in America, he told us, and his wife had just picked him up from the Nice airport. She had not been expecting him back so soon, and was just getting dressed to go out with her friends when he'd called from the airport. So that was why she was wearing that evening gown and fur coat.

"Every now and then I have to take a trip to the United States," he explained.

She too came across as somehow adrift. From the martini she had drunk in a single gulp? Or was it the dreamy, eccentric side of the English character? Again the image came to mind of Sylvia and me preparing an invisible spiderweb. They had entered the web while in a state of least resistance. I tried to recall how they had burst into the café. They had had a disoriented look on their faces, a staggering walk, hadn't they?

■

"I don't think I'm up to going to your friends' house," Neal said to his wife.

"It doesn't matter. I'll just cancel with them."

He gulped down a third coffee. "That's better. It really is nice to be back on solid ground. I hate flying."

Sylvia and I exchanged a look. We didn't know if we should say goodbye or stay with them. Did they want to get to know us better?

The lights in the glassed-in café went out with a click of a switch, but those in the restaurant room stayed on, leaving us in semidarkness.

"It looks like they're trying to tell us something," Neal said.

He rummaged in his jacket pockets.

"Damn. I don't have any French money."

I started to pay for our drinks, but Neal's wife had already taken a wad of bills out of her handbag and negligently put one down on the table.

Neal stood up. In the dim light, fatigue cut lines into his face.

"We need to go home. I'm about to fall over."

His wife took his arm and we followed them.

■

Their car was parked a little way off down the Promenande des Anglais, by the Iranian bank that, judging from its dusty window, had been closed for a long time.

"I'm so glad to have met you," Neal told us. "But it's funny, I feel like we've met before."

And he stared at Sylvia. That I remember very well.

"Do you want us to drop you off somewhere?" his wife asked.

I told them it wasn't worth the trouble. I was afraid we wouldn't be able to get rid of them. I thought about those drunks who cling to you and try to get you into every bar for one last drink. They get aggressive sometimes. But what did the Neals have in common with such vulgar types? They were calm and sophisticated.

"Where are you staying?" Neal asked.

"Off Boulevard Gambetta."

"That's our street," his wife said. "We can drop you off, if you want, it's no trouble."

"Yes," Sylvia said.

I was surprised at her decisive tone. She took my arm as though trying to drag me into the Neals' car against my will. We ended up in the back seat, with Neal's wife driving.

"I'd rather you drive," Neal said. "I'm so tired I might send you flying through the windshield."

We drove past the Queenie, where all the lights were now out, then the Palais de la Méditerranée. Its arcades were fenced off, the windows dark, blinds down, as though the building was about to be demolished.

"Are you living in an apartment?" Neal's wife asked.

"No, we're staying in a hotel at the moment."

She had taken advantage of a red light at Rue de Cronstadt to turn back toward us. She smelled a little like pine, and I wondered if it was her skin or her fur coat.

"We live in a villa," Neal said, "and we would be delighted to have you come over."

Exhaustion made his voice sound thick and his slight foreign accent was more audible.

"Are you staying in Nice long?" Mrs. Neal asked.

"Yes, we're here on vacation," I said.

"Do you live in Paris?" Neal asked.

Why were they asking all these questions? Back at the café they had not shown the least bit of curiosity about our situation. I felt increasingly uneasy. I wanted to give Sylvia a sign. We would get out of the car at the next red light. But what if the doors were locked?

"We live near Paris," Sylvia said.

Her calm tone of voice made my fears evaporate. Neal's wife turned on the windshield wipers, since it was still raining, and their regular movement reassured me as well.

"Anywhere near Marnes-la-Coquette?" Neal asked. "My wife and I used to live in Marnes-la-Coquette."

"No," Sylvia said. "We lived east of Paris, along the Marne."

She said it defiantly, like a challenge, and smiled at me. Her hand slid into mine.

"I don't know that area at all," Neal said.

"It has its own particular charm," I said.

"Where, exactly?" Neal asked.

"La Varenne-Saint-Hilaire," Sylvia said in a clear voice.

And why shouldn't we answer their questions perfectly naturally? Why should we lie to them?

"But we're not planning to go back," I added. "We want to stay on the Riviera."

"Good decision," Neal said.

I was relieved. We hadn't spoken to anyone for such a long time that we were starting to circle around in this city like animals in a cage. But no, we weren't contagious, we could have a normal conversation with someone, even make new friends.

The car turned down Rue Caffarelli, and I pointed out the gate of the Sainte-Anne to Mrs. Neal.

"That's not a hotel," Neal said.

"No, it's a furnished pension."

I was immediately sorry I said it, since it might awaken their suspicions. Maybe they had a prejudice against people who lived in furnished rooms.

"Is it nice there?" Neal asked.

Apparently it didn't bother them; if anything, they seemed to feel a certain sympathy for us.

"It's only temporary," Sylvia said. "We're hoping to find something else."

The car had stopped in front of the Sainte-Anne. Mrs. Neal turned off the motor.

"We might be able to help you find another place to live," Neal said absentmindedly. "Don't you think, Barbara?"

"Of course," Mrs. Neal said. "We'll have to see you again."

"Let me give you our address," Neal said. "Call us whenever you want."

He took a wallet out of his pocket and a card out of the wallet, and handed it to me.

"Goodbye . . . Hope to see you soon."

Mrs. Neal had turned to face us. "It was very nice to meet you."

Did she mean it? Or was she just being polite?

They looked at us in silence, in the same position, turned to face us. I didn't know what to say and Sylvia didn't either. I think that they would have thought it was perfectly normal for us to stay in the car and that it didn't matter to them. They would have agreed to whatever we proposed. It was up to us to decide. I opened the door.

"Goodbye," I said. "And thanks for the ride."

Before opening the gate, I turned back toward them and glanced at their car's license plate. The letters CD made my heart skip a beat: they stood for CORPS DIPLOMATIQUE but for a second I confused it with the license plates of police cars and thought we had been caught in a trap.

"We borrowed the car from some friends," Neal said, sounding amused.

He leaned his head out the open car window and smiled at me. He must have noticed my surprised expression on seeing his license plate. I was already pushing on the gate but it didn't budge. I turned the handle again and again and finally gave the gate a shove with my shoulder, and it opened abruptly.

We closed it behind us and couldn't help but look back at them one more time. They were sitting in the car, next to each other, frozen in place, like statues.

■

When we got back to the room it had the same musty smell. Usually when we came back at the end of another empty day, we felt such loneliness that the moisture and moldy smell went right through us. We would press close together on the bed, whose frame and bedsprings squeaked; eventually, it felt like the odor had seeped into our skins. We had bought sheets that we perfumed with lavender. But the smell never left.

That night, everything was different. For the first time since we had arrived in Nice, we had broken out of the magic circle keeping us isolated, strangling us little by little. Suddenly the room seemed temporary. We didn't even need to open the windows to air it out, or wrap ourselves in the lavender-scented sheets. We could keep the smell at a distance.

I pressed my forehead against the window and waved Sylvia over to me. Beyond the garden fence, the Neals' car was still parked with the motor off. What were they talking about? What were they waiting for? That gray, motionless car—was it some kind of threat to us? Well, we would see how things went. Anything would be better than this lethargy we had fallen into.

The motor started, and after another long moment the car pulled out and disappeared around the corner of Rue Caffarelli and Avenue Shakespeare.

Now I'm sure of it: Villecourt turned up after we first met the Neals. The event took place the following week. We hadn't seen the Neals again, because a good ten or twelve days went by before we could reach them by phone and set up a time to meet.

Event: here, too, it's the wrong word. All we had to do was wait for Villecourt to cross our path.

On sunny mornings, we used to read our newspapers on a bench in the Jardin d'Alsace-Lorraine, near the slide and the swings. There, at least, we wouldn't be noticed. For lunch we'd have sandwiches in a café on Rue de France. Then we'd take a bus up to Cimiez or down to the port and stroll through the grass of the Jardin des Arènes or down the streets of the old town. Around five o'clock, we'd buy used mystery novels on Rue de France. Since the prospect of going back to the Sainte-Anne oppressed us, our steps always led us down to the Promenade des Anglais.

The fences and palm trees in the Masséna Museum garden, framed by the bay window, are silhouetted against the sky. The crystalline blue sky or the pink sky of sunset. The palm trees slowly turn into shadows, before the streetlight on the corner of the Promenade and Rue de Rivoli shines a cold light on them. Again I go into the bar through the massive wooden door on

Rue de Rivoli, so I won't have to cross the hotel lobby. And I sit facing the bay window. Just as on that night with Sylvia. We wouldn't take our eyes off that bay window. The bright sky and the palm trees contrasted with the semidarkness of the bar. But after a while, I would feel uneasy, like I was suffocating. We were trapped in an aquarium, looking through the glass at the sky and the vegetation outside. We would never breathe in the open air again. It came as a relief when night fell, darkening the window. Then all the lights in the bar would come on, and under the bright lights my nervousness would disappear.

Behind us, all the way in back, an elevator's metal door slid slowly open and let out hotel guests coming down from their rooms. They would sit at the bar tables. Every time, I would watch them appear and glide slowly and silently past, the way I would follow the movements of a clock, reassuring in their regularity.

The metal door opened to reveal a silhouette in a dark-gray suit that I recognized at once. I didn't even dare make a sign with my head to Sylvia, so that she, too, would see who was coming out of the elevator: Villecourt.

■

He turned away from us and headed toward the hotel lobby. He passed the entrance to the bar and there was no more risk that he would see us. I whispered to Sylvia: "He's here."

She kept her cool, as though prepared for this eventuality. I was too, for that matter.

"I'll go see if it's really him."

She shrugged, as though it wouldn't make a difference.

I crossed the lobby and looked out the glass front door. He was standing on the sidewalk, on the corner of the Promenade des Anglais and Rue de Rivoli, where the large rental cars are parked. He was talking to one of the drivers. He took something out of his pocket but I couldn't see what it was—a notebook? a photograph? Was he asking the driver for an address? Or showing him photos of us, hoping the weasel-faced driver would remember having seen us?

In any case, the driver nodded and Villecourt slipped him a tip. Then he crossed the street at the light. He walked nonchalantly away down the Promenade, to the left, toward Jardin Albert I.

■

From the phone booth on Boulevard Gambetta, I called the Negresco Hotel.

"May I speak to Monsieur Villecourt, please?"

After a moment, the concierge replied: "There's no one by the name of Villecourt staying here."

"Yes there is. I just saw him at the bar. He was wearing a dark-gray suit . . ."

"Everyone wears dark-gray suits, sir."

I hung up.

"He's not staying at the Negresco," I said to Sylvia.

"It doesn't matter."

Had he given special instructions to the concierge? Or registered under another name? It was terrible to not be able to fix him in place, to feel that he might be lurking around every corner.

We had dinner in the café next to the Forum Cinema. We'd decided to act as though Villecourt did not pose any danger to us. If, by any chance, we met him and he wanted to talk to us, we would pretend we didn't know him. Pretend? We just had to convince ourselves that we were different people than the Jean and Sylvia who, once upon a time, had haunted the banks of the Marne. We had nothing in common with those two anymore. And Villecourt wouldn't be able to prove otherwise. To start with, Villecourt: he was nothing.

After dinner, we looked for an excuse not to go back to our room right away. We bought two balcony tickets for the Forum Cinema.

And before the lights went out in the theater full of old red velvet, before the local ads were moved aside to reveal the screen, we signaled to the usher for her to bring us two ice creams.

But when we left, I felt the vague presence of Villecourt. It was like the musty smell in our room — something we would never get rid of. It stuck to our skin. Sylvia sometimes used to call Villecourt "the clingy Russian," since he said that his father was Russian. Another lie.

We walked slowly back up Boulevard Gambetta, on the left-hand sidewalk. Passing the phone booth, I felt like calling the

Neals. No one had answered when I'd called there before. Maybe we'd always tried at a bad time, or maybe they'd left Nice. I would have been almost shocked if they did answer, they were so hazy and mysterious in my memory. Were they real? Were they nothing but a mirage, brought about by our extreme solitude? It would have been a comfort to hear a friendly voice. They would make Villecourt's presence in Nice less oppressive.

"What are you thinking about?" Sylvia asked me.

"The 'clingy Russian.'"

"Who cares about the Russian."

The gentle slope of Rue Caffarelli. No cars. No sound. Still some villas among the apartment buildings, and one of them, which looked somehow Florentine, surrounded by a large lawn. But there was a construction company sign on the gate saying that the villa was about to be torn down to make room for a luxury apartment building. One of the "model apartments" was already open for viewing at the back of the garden. I read on a crumbling marble sign: "Villa Bezobrazoff." Russians had lived there.

I showed Sylvia the sign: "Do you think that was Villecourt's family?"

"We'd have to ask him."

"Perhaps," I said in a solemn, chamberlain's voice, "the elder Villecourt used to take his afternoon tea at the Bezobrazoffs' when he was a boy . . ." Sylvia laughed.

There was still a light on in the pension lobby. We walked as quietly as we could, so as not to make the gravel crunch. I had left the windows open in the room, and the scent of wet leaves and honeysuckle was mixed in with the moldy smell. But little by little, the mold won out.

The diamond twinkled on her neck in the light of the moon. How hard and cold it was compared to her soft skin, how indestructible against her slender, touchingly fragile body . . . More than the room's smell, more than Villecourt prowling around us, that diamond glittering in the half light suddenly became in my eyes the blazing sign of the evil fate hanging over us. I wanted to take it off her, but I couldn't find the clasp on the chain at the back of her neck.

The incident occurred two days later, under the arcades on Place Masséna.

We were walking back from Jardin Albert I when we ran into Villecourt. He was coming out of a newsstand wearing the same dark-gray suit I had seen him in at the hotel bar. I immediately turned my head and pulled Sylvia away, holding her arm tight.

But he had recognized us among all the people walking by on that Saturday afternoon. He headed toward us, pushing his way through the people separating us, his eyes wide, gaze fixed on us. He was in such a hurry that he let drop the newspapers he'd been holding, folded, under his arm.

Sylvia made me slow down. She seemed perfectly calm.

"You're scared of the Russian?"

She forced herself to smile. We turned onto Rue de France. He was thirty or forty feet behind us, blocked by a group of tourists leaving a pizzeria. Then he caught up.

"Jean . . . Sylvia . . ."

He spoke in a fake-friendly voice but we kept walking, ignoring him. He fell into step with us.

"What, you don't want to talk to me? Don't be ridiculous."

He put a hand on my shoulder and then gripped harder and

harder. So I turned around. Sylvia too. We faced him and didn't move. He must have read something in my face that made him nervous, because he was looking at me with a kind of fear.

I would have squashed him like a cockroach if I could, of course. I would have felt like a swimmer reemerging into the air.

"Well then. Not even a hello?"

Yes, if we had been alone I would definitely have killed him, one way or another, but we were in a pedestrian zone on Rue de France, in the middle of a Saturday afternoon, with more and more people around us who would have formed a crowd at the slightest incident.

"You don't recognize your old friends?"

Sylvia and I started walking faster. But he kept following us, sticking to us.

"Just five minutes, come have a drink. Let's have a little talk."

We hurried on. He caught up to us, passed us, and tried to block our path. He was hopping back and forth in front of us like a soccer player trying to steal the ball. His smile infuriated me.

I tried to push him aside with my arm but accidentally gave him a bloody lip with my elbow. I felt like something irreversible had happened. Passersby were already stopping to look at Villecourt, who had a trickle of blood on his chin. But he was still smiling.

"You won't give me the slip like that."

Now his tone was more aggressive. He kept hopping from one foot to the other in front of us.

"We still have some things to take care of, don't you think? If we don't, there're other people who will take care of them for us."

This time he was ready to come to blows. I pictured the people on the street in a circle around us, a circle we would never be able to break free of; someone would call the police and the police van would emerge from a cross street . . . That must have been Villecourt's plan.

I shoved him again. Now he was walking alongside us, at the same rapid pace. The blood dripped from the bottom of his chin.

"We need to talk. I have a lot of things to tell you."

Sylvia took my arm and we tried to move away, but he stuck to us like a leech.

"You can't just ignore me, I exist too. There are problems we need to take care of, or else other people will get involved . . ."

He grabbed my wrist with a grip that he tried to make seem friendly. I gave him a sharp elbow in the side to get free. He grunted.

"You really want me to make a fuss on the street? You want me to start screaming 'Stop, thief!'?"

He grinned a strange grin, twisting his whole face.

"You'll see me everywhere. Let's at least try to talk it out. That's the only way to keep the others from getting involved."

We broke into a run. He was caught by surprise and we got a big head start. He pushed someone aside and ran after us, but two men stepped in and challenged him. We rushed through a carriage door, down an alleyway, and through a courtyard, making it back to the Promenade des Anglais.

■

In the phone booth on Boulevard Gambetta I dialed the Neals'
number again. It rang and rang without anyone answering. We
didn't want to go back to the pension and were hoping the Neals
would invite us over. There we would be out of Villecourt's reach.

But after a while, on the sunny sidewalk, amid the groups of
people strolling past toward the sea, the whole incident started to
seem faintly ridiculous. There was no need to take precautions.
We could enjoy this mild winter day the same as everybody else.
Villecourt, despite all his efforts, would not be able to meddle in
our new life. He was a thing of the past.

"But why was he hopping up and down in front of us?" Sylvia
asked me. "He wasn't acting normal."

"No. He didn't seem normal."

The way he was following us, the threats he was making without seeming to entirely believe them himself, showed how much
weaker he had become. He was hardly real anymore. Even the
blood that had spurted from his lip and covered his chin seemed
less like real blood than a special effect in a movie. And it was a
bit disconcerting how easily we had gotten away from him.

We picked a bench in the sun in the Jardin d'Alsace-Lorraine.
Children were sliding down the green slide, others playing in the
sandbox, still others astride the seesaw going up, down, up, in a
movement as regular as a metronome that eventually numbed us.
If Villecourt passed by here, he wouldn't spot us among all the
people watching their children. And even if he did, so what? We

were no longer in the murky environment along the banks of the Marne, with the stench of mud rising up from the stagnant water. The sky was too blue, that afternoon, the palm trees too tall, the buildings too pink and too white—a ghost like Villecourt could never withstand the summer colors. They would finish him off. He would vanish into the air with its lingering scent of mimosa.

I sometimes walk past the villa where the Neals lived. It's on Boulevard de Cimiez, on the right, some hundred and fifty feet before the corner with the old Regina Hotel looming over it. It's one of the few detached houses surviving in the neighborhood. But doubtless these vestiges will be gone soon too. Nothing can stand in the way of progress.

I was thinking about it the other morning, coming back from a walk I had taken up the hill to Cimiez, all the way to the Jardin des Arènes. I'd stopped in front of the villa. For some time a building had been going up in the abandoned part of the garden. I wondered if they would eventually tear down the villa itself, or preserve it, as a side building to the new one. It had a chance to survive: it wasn't run-down at all, and it looked a little like a 1930s-style Petit Trianon, with its arched French windows.

You could hardly see it because it overhung the boulevard; to see it properly over the high wall with its railing you had to stand on the opposite side of the street, at the corner of Avenue Édouard VII. An entrance with a cast-iron gate was cut into the base of the wall, and behind it a grand stone staircase led up the side of the embankment to the stone landing.

The gate is always open to give access to the construction

site. There is a white sign on the wall giving the name of the construction company, the architect's firm, the management company, and the date of the permit. The new building will be named after the villa: Château Azur. Proprietor: S.E.F.I.C., Rue Tonduti-de-l'Escarène, Nice.

I went to that address one day to find out the name of the person from whom S.E.F.I.C. corporation had bought Château Azur. I was given information I knew already—the villa, among other buildings, had belonged to the American embassy, which had rented it out. I realized that further efforts would seem inappropriate, even suspect, to the company's agent who was talking to me, a friendly blond man. So I didn't press the matter further.

And why bother? Even before S.E.F.I.C. acquired Château Azur and started building, I had spent a long time trying to find out about it. Just as in the office on Rue Tonduti-de-l'Escarène, my questions had remained unanswered.

Almost seven years before, the villa still looked unchanged. No construction site, no sign on the large railed wall. The entrance gate was closed. Parked on the sidewalk was the gray car with the CD plates, the same car the Neals had used to drive Sylvia and me back to the Sainte-Anne Pension on the night we'd met. I rang the bell at the gate. A brown-haired man, about forty, in a navy blue suit, appeared:

"What do you want?" he said rudely, with a Parisian accent.

"I recognized my friends' car," I said, pointing to the gray automobile. "I wanted to say hello."

"Who?"

"Mr. Neal."

"I'm afraid you're mistaken. That is Mr. Condé-Jones's car."

He stayed behind the gate and watched me closely, trying to tell if I posed any danger.

"You're sure," I said, "that it's his car?"

"Absolutely sure. I'm his chauffeur."

"But my friend lived here."

"I'm afraid you're mistaken, sir. This house belongs to the American embassy."

"But my friend's American . . ."

"The American consul lives here. Mr. Condé-Jones."

"Since when?"

"Since six months ago."

He looked at me from behind the gate as though I were a little crazy.

"Could I speak to the consul?"

"Do you have an appointment?"

"No, but I'm an American citizen and I need to ask him about something."

The American citizenship I had given myself made him suddenly trust me.

"In that case, you can see Mr. Condé-Jones now, if you want. It's his visiting hours."

He opened the gate and stepped aside with all the respect due an American citizen. Then he led me up the stairs.

On a white wooden chair next to the empty swimming pool in front of the house, a man sat smoking, his face turned slightly to one side, as though he were trying to expose it to the sun's weak rays. He did not hear us approaching.

"Mr. Condé-Jones . . ."

The man looked up at us and gave an attentive smile.

"Mr. Condé-Jones, this gentlemen wishes to see you. He is an American citizen."

At that he stood up. A short man, fat, black hair combed back, a moustache, big blue eyes.

"What can I do for you?" he asked in French, without a trace of an accent, in a voice so gentle it was like a balm to my soul. The phrase he'd used expressed not just politeness but a tactful attentiveness. At least that's what I thought I heard in his voice. And it had been a long time since anyone had asked me what they could do for me.

"I was just looking for some information," I mumbled.

The chauffeur had withdrawn, and it felt strange finding myself by the side of this pool.

"What kind of information?"

He looked at me kindly.

"I lied to get in to see you . . . I said I was American."

"American or not, my friend, it doesn't matter."

"Well, I was looking for some information about the people who lived in this house before you."

"Before me?"

He turned around and shouted: "Paul!"

And the chauffeur appeared in an instant, as though he'd been hiding right next to us, behind a tree or a wall.

"Could you bring us something to drink?"

"Right away, sir."

Condé-Jones gestured for me to take a seat in one of the white wooden chairs, and sat down next to me. The chauffeur placed a tray at our feet with two glasses full of a milky liquid. Pastis? Condé-Jones took a big sip of his.

"Go ahead, I'm listening. Tell me everything."

He seemed happy to have company, no matter who. The position of consul in Nice clearly left him a lot of free time to fill.

"I used to come here a lot, a while ago. I was visiting a couple who said they owned this house."

There was no way I could tell him everything. I'd decided not to tell him about Sylvia.

"What were these friends' names?"

"The Neals. He was American and she was English. They also drove your car, the one parked on the street."

"That's not my car," Condé-Jones told me after downing the rest of his pastis. "It was there when I got here."

▪

But before long the car was gone. Every time I went up the hill to Cimiez, I hoped it would be parked in front of the villa. But it wasn't there. One afternoon I rang the bell, just to be sure of things. No one answered. I decided that Condé-Jones must have left, with his gray diplomat's car, and that no other consul had come to replace him at Château Azur. Later, the S.E.F.I.C.

company sign appeared on the railed wall, which meant that the villa no longer belonged to the American embassy and that there would surely not be any villa at all soon.

The last time I'd seen Condé-Jones, it was a late afternoon in April. I had left him my address and he had been kind enough to send me a note, inviting me over and saying he had ready for me all the information I wanted about Château Azur—information, he said, that I would find very interesting.

He was sitting in the same place as when we'd met: next to the empty swimming pool, its bottom lined with dead leaves and pine needles. I had the feeling he'd been there, without moving, ever since "assuming his duties"—as he'd put it once, with a little self-mockery. Even if he could boast the title of consul, his "duties" in Nice were rather vague. He knew that the post was nothing but a place to park someone relegated to waiting for his official retirement date.

And now the date had come. He was heading back to America after more than twenty years of faithful service to the U.S. embassy in France. He had wanted me to come by that day so that he could give me the information I was interested in, but also to "raise a glass in farewell" (he often used idioms that he got slightly wrong).

"I'm leaving tomorrow," he said. "I'll give you my address in Florida, and if you ever happen to be visiting there, I would be delighted to see you."

He was especially kind to me, even though we had seen each other only three or four times since the day I had rung the bell at the gate of his villa—maybe I was the only person who had ever intruded on his diplomatic solitude.

"I'm sorry to be leaving the Riviera."

He cast a thoughtful glance at the empty pool and the overgrown garden smelling of eucalyptus.

The chauffeur had brought us a drink. We were seated side by side.

"Here's all your information." He handed me a large blue envelope. "I had to ask the embassy in Paris."

"Thank you so much for taking all that trouble."

"Not at all. I found it very instructive . . . You should read that document very carefully. It's worth your time."

I put the envelope on my lap. He gave me an ironic smile.

"You did say that your friend was named Neal, right?"

"Yes."

"How old was he?"

"About forty."

"That's what I thought. It's a real case of . . ." And he paused, looking for the right word. He spoke perfect French but every now and then—probably a typical diplomat's habit—he hesitated, looking for the most precise term.

"A case of revenants."

"Revenants?"

"Yes, back from the dead. You'll see."

To be polite, I didn't want to open the envelope in front of him. He was drinking his pastis in big sips, contemplating the garden before us bathed in the last rays of sunlight.

"I'll be bored in America. I've grown to like this house. A very strange house, though, if you believe what it says in that document. Anyway, I never heard anything suspicious while I was here. Never saw any ghosts in the night. I have to admit, though, I am a very heavy sleeper . . ."

He gave me a friendly pat on the arm.

"You're right to want to find out more about the mysteries of these old houses along the Riviera, my friend."

■

Inside the envelope were two sheets of paper, the same blue color, with the letterhead of the American embassy. The information, gathered and typed in orange characters, was as follows: Château Azur, Boulevard de Cimiez, had belonged in the 1930s to one E. Virgil Neal, American citizen, owner of Tokalon perfume and beauty products, with offices in Paris (7 Rue Auber and 138 Rue de la Pompe) and New York (27 W. 20th Street). In 1940, at the start of the Occupation, Neal had returned to America but his wife had stayed in France. "Mme Virgil Neal, née Bodier, as a French citizen, had been able to take over her husband's business, the Tokalon perfume and beauty product company, and avoid provisional confiscation by the German authorities after the United States entered the war."

The situation had grown more complicated in September 1944, due to the fact that "Mme Virgil Neal had maintained very close relations during the German Occupation, in Paris and on the Riviera, with one Ladd, André, b. 30 June 1916, last known place of residence 53 Avenue George-V, Paris VIIIe, convicted in absentia on 21 March 1948 of passing intelligence to the enemy and sentenced to no less than twenty years hard labor, twenty years exile, confiscation of all goods and property, and loss of full citizenship rights."

The embassy's report stated that the Château Azur villa had been sequestered in September 1944, "following a French federal investigation of the man known as Ladd, André, intimate of Mme Virgil Neal." The villa was then requisitioned by the American army. An agreement followed in July 1948, according to which "M. Virgil Neal, chief executive of Tokalon, Manufacturing Chemists and Perfumers, transferred ownership of his villa, Château Azur, to the American embassy in France."

The report also specified that "M. and Mme Virgil Neal had no children." Condé-Jones had underlined this sentence in green ink and written in the margins: "There are only two possibilities. Either your friends were revenants, or else Monsieur and Madame Virgil Neal possess an elixir of eternal youth manufactured in the labs of Tokalon, Manufacturing Chemists and Perfumers. I am counting on you to solve the mystery. Best regards."

But I wasn't dreaming. His name really was Virgil Neal. I'd kept the card he gave me at our first meeting, where he'd written his phone number at the villa. In the phone booth on Avenue Gambetta, I used to take the card out of my pocket before dialing the number. I checked it again last night—it really was embossed with the names, without any address: Monsieur and Madame Neal.

The only evidence of our having met the Neals—but can I call them that, without believing, as Condé-Jones suggested, in either revenants or fountains of youth?—the only remaining proof that I wasn't dreaming are that card and a photograph of the four of us, the Neals and Sylvia and me, taken by one of the photographers who wander up and down the Promenade des Anglais, waiting for tourists.

I still run into him every time I walk past his post at the old Palais de la Méditerranée. He greets me but doesn't raise his camera toward me. He must realize that I'm not a tourist, that I'm part of the landscape, practically blending in with the city.

The day he took our picture, neither Sylvia nor the Neals noticed him. He slipped his brochure into my hand. I went to pick up the picture three days later in a little shop on Rue de

France, without even telling Sylvia. I always go pick up that kind of photograph—traces left by an ephemeral moment when a person was happy, taking an afternoon stroll in the sun . . . You shouldn't underestimate these sentinels with their cameras on straps, ready to capture you in an instant—these guardians of memory patrolling the streets. I know what I'm talking about. I used to be a photographer myself.

I want to write down the details of our relations with the Neals as though writing up a police report or answering questions from a well-intentioned detective, someone looking out for me, with a paternal solicitude I can feel, trying to help me clear things up a little.

I must have reached this Virgil Neal by phone during the week that followed Villecourt's reappearance. He was "delighted" to hear from us, he said. He and his wife had been out of town for two weeks "on an unexpected business trip." But they would be "thrilled" to see us for lunch, as early as the next day, if that would work for us. He gave me the address of the restaurant where we should meet them between twelve and twelve-thirty.

It was an Italian restaurant with a garnet-colored roughcast façade on Rue des Ponchettes, at the foot of Château Rock. Sylvia and I were the first to arrive. We were seated at the table for four that Neal had reserved. No other customers. Crystal. Starched white napkins. Guardi-style paintings on the walls. Cast-iron grates on the windows. An enormous fireplace, with a fleurs-de-lys escutcheon carved inside on the back. Invisible loudspeakers were playing orchestral versions of popular songs.

I think Sylvia felt the same apprehension as me. We didn't actually know anything about these people who had invited us to lunch. Why did Neal seem to be in such a hurry to see us again? Was it that warmth and familiarity that Americans often demonstrated at a first meeting, calling you by your first name and showing you pictures of their children?

When they came they apologized for being late. Neal was a different man than the one from the other night. He no longer seemed adrift; he was freshly shaven and wearing a loose-fitting tweed jacket. He talked without any hesitation or trace of an American accent, and his volubility, if I remember correctly, was the first thing to rouse my suspicions. It seemed strange for an American. In certain slang words he used, in the turn he gave to certain phrases, I detected a mixture of Parisian intonations and an accent from the south of France—but held back, reined in, as if Neal had spent a long time keeping it hidden. His wife spoke much less than he did, and with the same dreamy, somewhat absentminded air that had surprised me the first time. The way she talked didn't sound English either. I couldn't help saying to them: "You speak such perfect French. It's hard to believe you're not from France . . ."

"I went to a French-language school," he said, "and spent my whole childhood in Monaco. My wife, too. That's where we met."

She nodded in agreement.

"What about you?" he suddenly asked. "What did you do in Paris?"

"I was an art photographer."

"Art photographer?"

"Yes. I'm planning to continue that line of work here in Nice."

He seemed to be considering what the profession of art photographer might be. He eventually said: "Are you married?"

"Yes, we're married," I said, giving Sylvia a fixed stare. But she didn't react to my lie at all.

I don't like it when people ask me questions. Besides, I wanted to find out more about them. To evade Neal's suspicions, I turned to his wife and said, "So, did you have a nice trip?"

She was embarrassed and hesitated before answering. Neal, though, said very smoothly: "Yes . . . A business trip."

"What sort of business?"

The abrupt way I asked the question surprised him.

"Oh . . . It's about a perfume deal I'm trying to set up between France and the U.S. I'm working with a small manufacturer in Grasse."

"Have you been doing that long?"

"No, no . . . Just in my spare time."

He had said that last sentence a bit arrogantly, as if wanting me to know that he didn't need to work for a living.

"We've even invented some new beauty products. It's fun for Barbara . . ."

Neal's wife had found her smile again.

"Yes, I'm interested in the whole beauty product side," she said in her dreamy voice. "I'm happy to leave the perfumes to Virgil. What I want is to set up a beauty salon here on the Riviera . . ."

"We're not sure where exactly," Neal said. "I think somewhere not too close to Monaco. I don't know if that kind of salon would work in Nice . . ."

When I remember this conversation, I'm sorry I didn't have

the information Condé-Jones was to give me later. What a face Neal would have made if I had said, in a suave voice, "So, you're relaunching Tokalon?"

And then, leaning my face close to his: "You're the same Virgil Neal as the one from before the war?"

■

Sylvia had a kind of obsession with putting the diamond in her mouth and keeping it between her lips, as if sucking a hard candy. Neal was sitting across from her and the gesture had not escaped him.

"Careful, it'll melt."

But he wasn't only joking around. The moment Sylvia relaxed her lips and the diamond fell back onto her black sweater, I noticed the attentive eye Neal fixed on the stone.

"That's a nice stone you have there," he said with a smile. "Don't you think, Barbara?"

She had turned her head, and she too was examining the diamond.

"Is it real?" she asked in a childish voice.

Sylvia and I exchanged glances.

"Yes, unfortunately it is," I said.

Neal seemed surprised at my answer.

"Are you sure? The size is impressive."

"It's a family jewel my wife's mother gave her," I said. "It's more of a hassle for us than anything else."

"You've had it appraised?" Neal asked in a tone of polite curiosity.

"Oh, yes. We have a whole dossier about it. It's called the Southern Cross."

"You can't wear it around like that," Neal said. "If it's real . . ."

Apparently he didn't believe me. Of course, who would have? People don't casually wear diamonds of that size and clarity. They don't hold them between their lips before letting them drop onto their black sweater. They don't suck them.

"My wife keeps it on her because we don't have anything else we can do."

Neal furrowed his brow.

"What else should we do? Rent a safe-deposit box at a bank?" I said.

"When people see it on me, everyone thinks it's from Burma," Sylvia said.

"From Burma?"

Neal didn't know this argot for a fake.

"We really want to sell it," I said. "But the problem is, it's hard to find a buyer for a stone like this."

He looked thoughtful, not taking his eyes off the diamond.

"I think I can find you a buyer. But first it'd have to be appraised."

I shrugged. "That would be great, if you could find a buyer. But I don't think it'll be easy."

"I can find you a buyer. But you'll need to show me your dossier," Neal said.

"I get the feeling you still think it's from Burma," Sylvia said.

■

We left the restaurant. The car was parked on Quai des États-Unis, in front of the shivering old men squeezed onto benches, taking the sun. I recognized the diplomatic plates. Neal opened the car door.

"Come over for a coffee," he said.

I wanted to get rid of them. Just like that. I asked myself what they could really do to help us. But we couldn't just ditch them because of a passing mood, we had to stay the course. They were the only two people we knew in Nice.

Just like the first time, Sylvia and I sat in back. Neal drove slowly up Boulevard de Cimiez, and the drivers behind him honked their horns for him to let them pass.

"They're crazy," Neal said. "They always want to go faster."

One of the drivers yelled a flurry of curses at him as he passed the car.

"It's my diplomatic plates that make them angry. Plus I guess they have to hurry to get back to their offices on time."

He turned around to me.

"Have you ever worked in an office?"

The car stopped by a wall with a railing. Neal pointed: "That's the house up there. It has a commanding view. You'll see. It's a very nice house . . ."

I noticed the marble plaque over the gate that said: "Château Azur."

"My father named it," Neal said. "He had the house built before the war."

His father? That was reassuring.

Neal closed the gate with the turn of a key, we set foot in the garden that ran down to Boulevard de Cimiez, and we climbed the staircase. The villa, recalling the Trianon, struck me as luxurious.

"Barbara, could you get us some coffee please?"

I was surprised there was no butler in a house like this. Maybe another sign of American casualness. Despite being very rich, the Neals were clearly a little bohemian, and Mrs. Neal made the coffee herself. That was it, bohemian. But rich. At least that's what I tried to convince myself.

We sat on the white wooden chairs that I would see again in the same place a year later, when I first met Condé-Jones. But the swimming pool was not yet empty. Branches and dead leaves were floating on the surface of the murky water before us. Neal picked up a stone and skipped it across the water.

"We need to empty the pool and do something about the garden," he said.

It was in bad shape. Bushes obstructed the gravel walkways, which were overrun with weeds. The lawn was a wasteland, and off to one side there was a fountain basin cracked down the middle.

"If my father could see this, he wouldn't understand. But I don't have time to take care of the garden." His voice sounded sad and sincere. "Everything was different in my father's day. Nice was a different city, too. Did you know that the police officers on the streets used to wear pith helmets?"

His wife put the tray down on the tiled floor. She had changed out of her dress into jeans. She poured the coffee and offered a cup to each of us in turn, with a graceful movement of her arms.

"Does your father still live here?" I asked Neal.

"My father is dead."

"I'm sorry."

He smiled to help me past my embarrassment. "I need to sell this house. But I can't bring myself to do it. It's so full of childhood memories. Especially the garden . . ."

Sylvia had nonchalantly headed toward the house, and she was pressing her forehead against one of the large French windows. Neal watched her with his face slightly tense, as though afraid she might discover something suspicious.

"I'll have to have you over once the house is all straightened up," he said in a loud, imperious voice. Maybe he wanted to keep her from walking through the half-open French doors into the house.

He walked over to her, put his arm around her shoulders, and brought her back to us by the pool. It was like he was fetching a child who had wandered away from a sandbox while his parents were distracted.

"We need to completely redo the house. I wouldn't want you to see it like this."

Seeing Sylvia far away from the French doors seemed to re-
assure him.

"We don't live here much at all, my wife and I. One or two
months a year at most."

I wanted to head over to the house myself, to see how Neal
would react. Would he physically prevent me? If he did, I would
lean over and whisper in his ear: "You seem like you're hiding
something in the house. What is it, a body?"

"My father has been dead for twenty years," Neal said. "As
long as he was here, everything was as it should be. The house
and the garden were impeccable. The gardener was an extraor-
dinary man . . ."

He shrugged, pointing to the shrubs and the walkways overrun with weeds.

"But now Barbara and I are going to be in Nice for a while.
Especially if we open that beauty salon. I'm going to fix this all
up."

"Where do you live most of the time?" Sylvia asked.

"London and New York," Neal replied. "My wife has a very
nice little house in London, in the Kensington area."

She was smoking and seemed to be ignoring her husband.

The four of us were sitting on the white wooden chairs in a
semicircle around the pool, each with a cup of coffee on the right
arm of the chair. The symmetry made me vaguely uneasy, once
I realized that it was not only due to the coffee cups. Barbara's
faded jeans were the exact same cut and color as Sylvia's, and
since they were sitting in the same relaxed pose, I could see that

they had the same narrow waists, emphasizing the curve of their hips in the same way, to the point where I wouldn't have been able to tell them apart just by looking at their waist and hips. I took a sip of coffee. Neal had raised his cup to his lips at the exact same moment, and our gestures of putting the cup back down on the arm of the chair were synchronized too.

The Southern Cross came up again that afternoon. Neal asked Sylvia, "So, you really want to sell your diamond?"

He leaned over to her and took the stone between his thumb and index finger, to examine it more closely. Then he gently placed it back onto her black sweater. I chalked it up to the offhand way Americans had. Sylvia hadn't budged an inch; she looked off in another direction as if trying to ignore Neal's gesture.

"Yes, we do," I said.

"If it's authentic, there won't be any problem."

He was obviously taking the matter seriously.

"Don't worry," I said in a condescending voice. "It's real. In fact, that's the concern. We don't want to keep such an important diamond."

"My mother gave it to me for my wedding and advised me to sell it," Sylvia said. "She always thought diamonds bring bad luck. She had tried to sell it herself but couldn't find an appropriate buyer."

"How much do you want for it?" Neal asked. Then he seemed

to regret having asked such a direct question, and forced himself to smile. "Sorry, I'm blunt that way. It's because of my father. He worked with a major American diamond dealer when he was young. That's where I got my taste for gemstones."

"We want about a million and a half," I said drily. "That's a very reasonable price for this diamond. It's worth twice that."

"We were planning to take it to Van Cleef's in Monte Carlo so they could find a buyer," Sylvia said.

"Van Cleef?" Neal repeated. The name, with its massive, dazzling glint, took him aback.

"I don't want to keep wearing it everywhere like a leash around my neck," Sylvia said.

Barbara Neal gave a sharp little laugh.

"Of course not. You're right," she said. "Someone might snatch it on the street."

And I wondered if she was serious or making fun of us.

"I can find you a buyer," Neal said. "Barbara and I know Americans in a position to buy it, don't we, darling?" He mentioned a few names, and she nodded in agreement.

"And you think they'll pay our price?" I said very softly.

"Definitely."

"Would you like something to drink?" Barbara Neal asked.

I glanced at Sylvia. I wanted to leave. But she seemed to be enjoying herself in this sunny garden, the back of her neck against the back of the chair, her eyes closed.

Barbara Neal headed toward the house. Neal gestured to Sylvia and asked me quietly: "Do you think she's asleep?"

"Yes."

He leaned toward me and said, in an even softer voice: "About the diamond . . . I think I might buy it myself, if you can give me proof it's authentic."

"It is."

"I want to give it to Barbara for our tenth anniversary."

He could see from my face that I was suspicious.

"Don't worry, I have plenty of money."

He grabbed my arm very tight, to make me understand that I needed to give him my whole attention: "It's not thanks to me—I was just born into the right family. I inherited a lot from my father. It's not fair, but that's how it is . . . Do you trust me now? You think I'm a serious customer?"

He laughed. Maybe he was trying to make me forget the aggressive tone with which he had made his proposal.

"We can't have any mistrust between us. I can make a down payment . . ."

■

Neal offered to drive us home, but I said we'd rather walk. Back on the Boulevard de Cimiez, I looked up and there they were, leaning on the balustrade, watching us. Neal waved. We had agreed to talk on the phone the next day and arrange a meeting. After a few steps I turned around again, and they hadn't moved, with their elbows on the railing.

"He wants to buy the diamond himself, to give to his wife," I said to Sylvia.

She didn't seem surprised. "For how much?"

"For what I said. Do you think they really have the money?"

We slowly walked down Boulevard de Cimiez in the brilliant sunshine. I took off my coat. I knew it was winter, that night was coming soon, but at that moment I would have thought it was July. The confusion of seasons, the few cars on the road, the sun, the shadows outlined so sharply on the sidewalk and the walls . . .

I grabbed Sylvia's wrist.

"Don't you feel like this is all a dream?"

She smiled at me but looked nervous.

"And you think that at some point we'll wake up?" she asked me.

We walked in silence to the bend in the road beneath the curved façade of the old Hotel Majestic, and took Boulevard Dubouchage back to the center of town. I was relieved to find myself back under the arcades on Place Masséna, in the noise of the crowd and the mass of people strolling or leaving work and waiting for the bus. All the hustle and bustle gave me an illusory sense of escaping from a dream that had been holding us prisoner.

■

A dream? It was more like the sensation of days following one after the other without our realizing, without any bumps or handholds that would let us catch them. We were advancing on a kind of moving walkway, and the streets slipped past, and we no longer knew whether the walkway was moving us, or we were motionless in a landscape sliding past all around us, like a scene in the movies shot with rear projection, or as it's called in French: *transparence*.

Sometimes the veil parted—never during the day, but at night, when the air was crisper and the lights sparkled. We walked along the Promenade des Anglais, making contact again with terra firma. The stupor we had felt since our arrival in this city dissipated. We felt masters of our destiny again. We could make plans. We would try to cross the Italian border. The Neals would help us do it. In their car with diplomatic plates we could enter Italy without passing through passport controls or attracting attention. We would travel south, to Rome, our goal, the only city where I imagined we would be able to settle for the rest of our lives—Rome, so perfect for natures as indolent as our own.

During the day, everything slipped through our fingers. Nice, with its blue sky, brightly colored buildings like gigantic frosted cakes or ocean liners, its deserted streets in the bright Sunday sun, our shadows on the sidewalks, the palm trees, the Promenade des Anglais—it all slipped past, like a rear projection. On the interminable afternoons when the rain beat on the tin roof, we would stay in the moist, musty smell of the room, feeling abandoned there. Later, I got used to the idea, and today I feel at ease in this city of ghosts where time has stopped. Like people passing in slow procession along the Promenade, I accept that I have lost a certain resilience. I am released from the law of gravity. I float like the other inhabitants of Nice. But back then, at the Sainte-Anne Pension, that state was new to us, and we still lurched this way and that to try to fight off the torpor overwhelming us. The only solid, consistent thing in our lives, the sole inalterable point of reference, was the diamond. Had it brought us bad luck?

We saw the Neals again. I remember meeting them at the bar of the Negresco Hotel one day at around three in the afternoon. We sat at a bay window waiting for them. It framed a patch of sky whose blue was much more distant and clear than this semidarkness we found ourselves in.

"What if Villecourt comes?"

I always called him by his family name.

"We'll act like we don't recognize him," Sylvia said. "Or else leave him with the Neals and disappear for good."

That word "disappear" in Sylvia's mouth sends chills up my spine today. But that afternoon I laughed at the thought of the Neals and Villecourt sitting at the same table, without knowing what to say to one another, growing more and more anxious at our prolonged absence.

Anyway, Villecourt did not come.

We took a walk with the Neals along the Promenade des Anglais. That was the day when the photographer stationed in front of the Palais de la Méditerranée raised his camera toward us and slipped a card into my hand giving the address of the store where we could go buy the photos of ourselves in three days.

The car with the diplomatic plates was parked by the Jardin

Albert I carousel. Neal told us that he was going to "hop over" to Monaco with his wife to "take care of some business." He was wearing a turtleneck sweater and the old suede jacket from the first night; Barbara Neal was in jeans and a sable-fur jacket.

Neal pulled me aside. We were in front of the slowly turning carousel. There was only one child, sitting on one of the red sleds being pulled by white wooden horses for all eternity.

"This reminds me of something from my childhood," Neal told me. "I must have been ten . . . yes . . . it was 1950 or '51. I was on a walk with my father and a friend of his. And I wanted to ride this carousel. My father's friend got on with me . . . Do you know what his name was, that friend of my father's? Errol Flynn. Does that name mean anything to you? Errol Flynn?"

He put his arm protectively around my shoulder.

"I wanted to talk to you about the diamond. It's almost Barbara's birthday. I'll give you a down payment as soon as I can. A check from my bank in Monaco. An English bank. Is that all right with you?"

"Whatever you want."

"I'll have the diamond set in a ring. Barbara will love it."

We rejoined Sylvia and Barbara. The Neals kissed us on the cheeks before getting in their car. They were a beautiful couple — so it seemed to me that day. And sometimes the air is so mild on the Riviera in winter, the sky and the sea so blue, life so easy on a sunny afternoon along the Villefranche corniche road, that anything seems possible: checks from an English bank in Monaco that someone stuffs into your pockets, Errol Flynn riding slowly round the carousel of the Jardin Albert I.

"Tonight we're taking you to dinner at Coco Beach!"

Neal's voice rang out on the phone. It had not the slightest American accent, even when he said the words "Coco Beach."

"We'll pick you up at your hotel sometime after eight."

"Why don't we meet out?"

"No, it's much easier to get you there. We might be a little late . . . Sometime after eight, at your hotel. We'll honk the horn."

There was no point in arguing. Never mind. I said it was fine. I hung up and stepped out of the phone booth on Boulevard Gambetta.

We left our room window open to hear the horn. We were both lying in bed, because that was the only piece of furniture in the room we could wait on.

It had started raining a few minutes before dusk—a soft rain, not beating on the tin roof but a kind of drizzle that gave us the illusion of being in a room in Le Touquet or Cabourg, in the north.

"Where is this Coco Beach?" Sylvia asked.

Near Antibes? Cap Ferrat? Or even farther? Coco Beach . . . The name had the sound and the scent of Polynesia, associated in my mind more with the beaches of Saint-Tropez: Tahiti, Morea . . .

"You think it's far from Nice?"

I was afraid of a long car ride. I never liked these late-night escapades hopping from one restaurant or nightclub to the next until, at the end of the night, you have to rely on the goodwill of one of your companions to drive you home, and he's drunk, and for the whole drive you're at his mercy.

"What if we stand them up?" I said to Sylvia.

We would turn off the lights in the room. They would push open the gate of the Saint-Anne Pension and cross the lawn. The owner would open the French doors to the lobby. Their voices on the veranda. Someone knocking repeatedly on our door. Our names being called. "Are you there?" Silence. Then would come the relief of hearing their steps get softer and farther away and the garden gate close. Alone at last. Nothing would equal that bliss.

Three blasts as loud as a foghorn. I leaned out the window and saw Neal's silhouette waiting outside the gate.

On the stairs, I said to Sylvia, "If Coco Beach is too far, we'll ask to stay in the neighborhood. We'll tell them we need to come home early because we're expecting a phone call."

"Or we'll just give them the slip," Sylvia said.

It had stopped raining. Neal waved his arm wildly. "I was afraid you hadn't heard the horn."

He was wearing a turtleneck sweater and his old suede jacket.

The car was parked on the corner of Avenue Shakespeare. A

black car, roomy, I didn't know what kind. German maybe. No diplomatic plates, but ones from Paris.

"I had to switch cars," Neal said. "The other one broke down."

He opened one of the doors for us. Barbara Neal was sitting in the front seat in her sable-fur jacket. Neal got behind the wheel.

"Next stop, Coco Beach!" he said, lurching into a U-turn.

He drove down Rue Caffarelli much too fast for my liking.

"Is it far?" I asked.

"Not far at all," Neal said. "Just past the port. It's Barbara's favorite restaurant."

She had turned to face us. She smiled at us, giving off her scent of pine trees.

"I'm sure you'll like it," she said.

We detoured around the port, and then passed Vigier Park and the Nautical Club. Neal turned off onto a winding street parallel to the coast. He stopped by a landing with a lit-up sign.

"Coco Beach, everybody out!"

There was a certain forced cheeriness in his voice. Why was he trying to play the clown that night?

We crossed the landing. Neal held his wife close and had his other arm around Sylvia's shoulders. A gust of wind blew and he said: "Careful, don't fall overboard!"

We went down a narrow staircase with a thick white braided cord for a banister, and over a gangway leading to the restaurant's main room. A maître-d' in a white outfit and yachtsman's cap appeared and said, "What name is your reservation under, sir?"

"Captain Neal!"

A large bay window ran the length of the room, which looked out over the sea some forty feet below. The sailor led us to a table next to the window. Neal wanted Sylvia and me to sit where we would have a panoramic view of Nice. A few scattered customers were talking in low voices.

"It's really busy here in summer," Neal said. "They take off the roof and make it al fresco. Would you believe it was my father's old gardener who built this restaurant, twenty years ago?"

"Is he still the owner?" I asked.

"No. Unfortunately. He's dead."

This answer disappointed me. My mood was not good that night, and I would have liked to meet Neal's father's former gardener. It would have reassured me that Neal really was from a rich and honorable American family.

Following the maître-d's lead, the waiters were dressed in white blazers with brass buttons and white pants, but no caps. There was a white life preserver above the entranceway with blue letters around the ring spelling "COCO BEACH."

"Great view, don't you think?" Neal said, suddenly twisting his body around.

The whole Baie des Anges lay spread out before our eyes, with its brightly lit areas and shadowy patches. Spotlights shone on the cliffs and the monument to the dead like a giant wedding cake at the foot of Château Rock. The Jardin Albert I down below was lit up, along with the white façade and pink dome of the Negresco.

"It feels like we're on a boat," Barbara said.

It was true. The crew in white moved smoothly and silently between the tables; I saw they were wearing espadrilles.

"You don't get seasick, do you?" Neal asked.

The question made me slightly anxious. Or was it the drops of rain on the windows and the wind, which was making the white flag clatter against the Coco Beach sign mounted on the pontoon in front of the restaurant like the prow of a yacht?

One of the waiters in white handed out menus.

"I recommend the bourride," Neal said. "Or, if you want, they make an aioli here like you'll never find anywhere else."

Americans are gourmands sometimes, and with their goodwill and their seriousness they can become well-informed connoisseurs of French cooking and French wine. But still, Neal's tone, the mimicry of his face, the sharp gesture of his thumb, and the way he had sung the praises of the bourride and the aioli made me think of very specific other places. I suddenly sensed coming from Neal the stench of La Canebière, or Pigalle.

■

Sylvia and I kept exchanging glances during the whole meal. I believe we were thinking the same thing: it would be so easy to ditch them there . . . But the idea of having to get back to the port stopped me. From the port, we could easily lose them in the streets of Nice, but to reach the port you had to walk down a long empty street and in their car they would easily catch up to us. They would stop and ask us to explain what we were doing. To answer them, to make excuses, or even to tell them to go to hell—none of that would help because they knew our address. I felt they were as clingy as Villecourt. No, it would be better to take things slow.

My bad mood worsened during dessert when Neal leaned over to Sylvia, brushed the diamond with his finger, and said: "So, still wearing your rock?"

"You learned argot at your school in Monaco?" I said.

His eyes narrowed and there was something hard in his look. "I was only asking your wife if she was still wearing her rock . . ."

Usually so friendly, he was suddenly aggressive. Maybe he'd had too much to drink during dinner. Barbara looked embarrassed and lit a cigarette.

"My wife is wearing a rock," I said, "but you can't afford it."

"Oh really?"

"I know it for a fact."

"Says who?"

"A little bird told me."

He gave a loud laugh. His gaze softened. Now he was looking at me with an amused expression.

"You're mad at me? I was just joking . . . a bad joke. I'm sorry."

"Me too, I was just kidding," I said.

There was a moment of silence.

"Well, if you were both joking," Barbara said, "then everything's fine."

He insisted we have some kind of plum or pear brandy, I'm not sure what. I brought the glass to my lips and pretended to take a sip. Sylvia drank hers in a single gulp. She had stopped talking and was nervously rubbing her "rock" between her fingers.

"You're mad at me too?" Neal asked her in a humble voice. "Over this thing with the rock?"

His faint American accent was back and he was a different person. There was something shy and charming about him now.

"I beg your pardon. I hope you'll forget my asinine joke."

He pressed the palms of his hands together in a childish pleading gesture.

"Do you forgive me?"

"I forgive you," Sylvia said.

"I'm truly sorry about that 'rock' thing . . ."

"Rock, no rock, I don't care," Sylvia said.

Now it was she who was talking in an east-Paris drawl.

"Is he often like that?" she asked Barbara, pointing to Neal.

She was taken aback, and eventually mumbled, "Sometimes."

"What do you do to calm him down?"

The question came down on the table like a guillotine. Neal laughed. "What a charming woman!" he said to me.

I felt uneasy. I took a large sip of the brandy.

"So how should we end the evening?" Neal said.

It was just what I'd predicted. Our troubles weren't over yet.

"I know a nice place in Cannes," Neal said. "We can have a glass of something there."

"In Cannes?"

Neal gave my shoulder a friendly pat. "Come on, old man, don't make such a face. Cannes is hardly a den of iniquity."

"We need to get back to our hotel," I said. "I'm expecting a phone call around midnight."

"Come on . . . Come on . . . You can call them yourselves, from Cannes. We won't let you go that easy."

I gave Sylvia a desperate look, but she was imperturbable. Eventually she came to my rescue.

"I'm tired. I don't feel like taking a long car ride tonight."

"A long car ride? To Cannes? You must be pulling my leg. Did you hear that, Barbara? A long car ride, to Cannes. They think it takes a long car ride to get to Cannes . . ."

Another word and we would have been in the presence of a jackhammer that would never stop clattering: "To Cannes, to Cannes . . ." And if we contradicted him he would cling to us even more than before. Why are some people like chewing gum that we have to try to get off our shoe heels by scraping them against the curb?

"I promise you we'll be in Cannes in ten minutes. The roads are empty at this time of night."

He didn't seem drunk. He was speaking in a quiet, normal voice. Sylvia shrugged. "Well, if you insist, let's go to Cannes."

She kept her cool and gave me an almost imperceptible wink.

"We'll talk about the diamond," Neal said. "I believe I've found you a buyer. Isn't that right, Barbara?"

She smiled without answering.

The waiters in white maneuvered between the tables, and I wondered how they could keep their footing so well. Outside the windows, the lights of Nice seemed farther and farther away, more and more blurry. We stepped out into the fresh air. Everything was swaying around me.

■

As we were getting into Neal's car, I said: "I'd really rather you take us back to our hotel . . . I don't want to miss that call."

He checked his watch, and his face broke into a large grin. "You're expecting a call at midnight? It's twelve-thirty. You have no more excuses for ditching us, old man . . ."

Sylvia and I took our seats in the back. Barbara snapped her gold cigarette case shut and turned to face us.

"You don't have a cigarette, do you?" she asked. I was out.

"Nope," Sylvia said rudely. "No cigarettes."

She had taken my hand and she pressed it against her knee. Neal started the car.

"Are you really going to insist on taking us to Cannes?" Sylvia asked. "Cannes is boring."

"You don't know what you're talking about," Neal said in a patronizing voice.

"We don't like nightclubs," Sylvia insisted.

"I'm not taking you to a nightclub."

"So where are we going, then?"

"It's a surprise."

He didn't drive as fast as I'd feared, and he turned on the radio with the volume low. Again we drove past the white Nautical Club building and Vigier Park. We were back at the port.

Sylvia squeezed my hand. I turned toward her. I tried to signal with a movement of my arm toward the door that we could get out of the car at the next red light. I think she understood because she nodded.

"I love this song," Neal said.

He turned up the volume on the radio and turned to face us. "Do you like it too?"

Neither of us answered. I was thinking about the route we would have to take to drive to Cannes. There would definitely be a red light by the Jardin Albert I. Or else farther up, at the Promenade des Anglais. The best thing for us would be to get out on the Promenade des Anglais and disappear into one of the side streets running off it, where Neal couldn't follow us because of the one-way streets.

"I'm out of cigarettes," Barbara said.

We had reached Quai Cassini. He stopped the car.

"You want us to stop and buy some?" Neal asked.

He turned to me.

"Would you mind going to buy some cigarettes for Barbara?"

He made a U-turn, then stopped again at the end of Quai des Deux-Emmanuel.

"You see the first restaurant on the quay? Garac? It's still open. Ask them for two packs of Cravens. If you run into any problems, just tell them it's for me. Madame Garac knew me as a child . . ."

I looked over at Sylvia. She seemed to be waiting for me to decide. I shook my head no — it was not yet the right moment to escape. It would be better to wait until we were in the center of Nice.

I tried to open the door but it was locked.

"Sorry," Neal said.

He pressed a button next to the gear shift. This time, the door opened.

I went into Garac and up the stairs leading to the restaurant. A blonde was standing behind the coat-check counter. A babble of conversations reached me from inside the restaurant.

"Do you have cigarettes?" I asked.

"What brand?"

"Craven."

"Ah, no. No English brands."

She showed me the tray with the cigarettes.

"It doesn't matter. I'll take Americans." I chose two packs at random and gave her a hundred francs. She opened one drawer, then another. She couldn't find the change.

"It doesn't matter," I told her. "Keep it."

I went down the stairs, and when I left the building the car was gone.

■

I waited on the sidewalk of Quai Cassini. Neal must have gone to get gas somewhere nearby and not found a station. The car would reappear before me any minute now. As more time passed, I felt increasingly panicked. I couldn't stand there waiting. I paced up and down the sidewalk. Eventually, when I looked at my watch, it was almost two o'clock in the morning.

A loud group of people left Restaurant Garac. Car doors slammed, engines started. Some people continued their conversations along the quay. I heard their voices and the sounds of their laughter. Down by the edge of the water, shadows were unloading crates and slowly stacking them near a pickup truck with its lights off and a tarp over the back.

I walked over to them. They were taking a break, leaning against the crates and smoking.

"You didn't see a car just now?" I asked.

One of them looked up at me. "What car?"

"A big black car."

I needed to talk to someone, not keep it all inside.

"Some friends were waiting for me in a black car, there, by the building. They left without telling me."

There was no point trying to explain. I didn't know what to say. Besides, they weren't listening. Still, one of them must have noticed my terrified face.

"A black car? What kind?" he asked.

"I don't know."

"You don't know the make of the car?"

He probably asked to see if I was drunk, or crazy. He looked at me suspiciously.

"No, I don't know the make of the car."

It was terrible not to know even that.

■

I walked up Boulevard de Cimiez. My heart had practically stopped. From a distance, I could make out the dark mass of a car parked in front of the balustraded wall of the Neals' villa. When I got closer I saw that it wasn't the car from earlier but the one with the diplomatic plates.

I rang the bell again and again. No one answered. I tried to push open the gate but it was locked. I crossed the street; the part of the house I could see over the wall was dark. I walked back down Boulevard de Cimiez and went into the phone booth at the bend in the road, by the Majestic. I dialed the Neals' number and let it ring for a long time. But no one answered, any more than they had at the gate. So I went back up to the villa again. The car was still there. I don't know why but I tried to open the car doors one by one; they were all locked. The trunk too. Then I rattled the gate, hoping it would open. No luck. I kicked the car, and then the gate, but there was nothing I could do. Everything was closed, I couldn't find any way in, make any contact with anything. It was all locked and sealed shut, forever.

■

Just like this city, through which I walked back to the Sainte-Anne Pension. Dead streets. Cars few and far between, and I looked at them all, one after the other, but none of them was the Neals'. They all seemed empty. Passing the Jardin d'Alsace-Lorraine, I saw a black car the same size as the Neals' stopped at the corner of Boulevard Gambetta. Its motor was running. Then it turned off. I went over to it but couldn't see anything through the tinted windows. I bent down and almost pressed my forehead against the windshield. A blonde was sitting sideways in the driver's seat, her breasts against the steering wheel and her back to a man trying to press himself against her. She seemed to be trying to fight him off. I had already started to walk away when a head appeared out a lowered window—a man with his dark hair combed back:

"Like what you see, you voyeur?"

Then a raucous laugh from the woman. Its echo seemed to follow me the whole length of Rue Caffarelli.

■

The gate of the Sainte-Anne Pension was locked and I thought I would never be able to get this one open either. But I braced myself and pushed with all my strength and eventually it opened. On the walk in the dark garden I had to feel my way to the back stairs.

When I went into the room and turned on the light, I felt comforted at first, since Sylvia's presence was still so vivid there. One of her dresses was draped over the back of the leather armchair; her other clothes were hanging in the wardrobe, her overnight bag still sitting there. Her toiletries hadn't vanished from the little white wooden table next to the sink. I couldn't resist taking a smell of her perfume.

I lay down on the bed, fully dressed, and turned off the light, with the idea that I'd be able to think better in the dark. But the darkness and silence enveloped me like a shroud, and I felt like I was suffocating. Little by little, this feeling gave way to one of emptiness and desolation. Being alone on that bed was unbearable. I turned on the bedside lamp and quietly told myself that it wouldn't be long before Sylvia was back in this room with me. She knew I was waiting for her. So I turned the lamp back off, the better to listen for the grinding noise of the gate when it opened and the sound of her footsteps coming down the path and up the steps.

■

I was nothing but a sleepwalker, moving back and forth from the Sainte-Anne Pension to the Neals' villa. I rang the bell for a long time without anyone answering. The car with the diplomatic plates was always parked in the same place, by the gate.

The Neals' number appeared in the Alpes-Maritimes phone book next to the listing: American Consulate Office, 50-*bis* Boulevard de Cimiez. I called the American embassy in Paris and asked them if they knew about a Virgil Neal living in one of their buildings, 50-*bis* Boulevard de Cimiez, Nice. I said he had disappeared overnight and that I was worried about him. No, they had never heard of any Virgil Neal. The Château Azur villa on Boulevard de Cimiez was a residence for embassy employees but had not been occupied for several months. An American consul was about to move in there. I would have to direct any further questions to him.

I read all the newspapers, especially those from the area, including the Italian ones. I went through the local news items with a fine-toothed comb. One of them jumped out at me. On the night Sylvia disappeared, a German car, an Opel, black, with Paris plates, had gone off the part of the road known as Chemin du Mont-Gros, between Menton and Castellar, and crashed into a ravine. It had caught fire. They had discovered two bodies in the car, charred beyond recognition.

I detoured down the Promenade des Anglais and went into a large garage, just before Rue de Cronstadt.

I asked one of the mechanics if he happened to have an Opel in the garage.

"Why?"

"Just because . . ."

He shrugged. "There, in the corner, all the way in the back."

Yes, it was the same kind of car as the Neals'.

■

I tried to revisit everywhere we had been with the Neals, hoping to find a trace, a thread that might lead me somewhere. Or maybe I would see them walk in with Sylvia, like in those movies that you have to rewind on the editing table to tirelessly reexamine the details of the same sequence. But the instant I'd walked out of Garac with the two packs of American cigarettes in my hand, the film strip had torn, or else reached the end of its reel.

Except for one night, in the Italian restaurant on Rue des Ponchettes where the Neals had arranged to meet us the first time.

I had chosen the same table as on that day, next to the giant fireplace, and the same chair. I was hoping that by returning to the same places, remaking the same gestures, I would eventually rejoin the invisible threads.

I had asked the woman who ran the restaurant and all the waiters if they knew the Neals. None of them recognized the name, even though Neal had told us he was a regular there. The customers were talking loud and the noise was oppressive, to the point where I no longer knew why I was there, or where I was.

The events of my life gradually blurred before dissolving altogether. There was nothing left but that moment, the people eating dinner, the giant fireplace, the imitation Guardis on the wall, and the murmuring of the voices . . . Nothing but that moment. I didn't have the courage to stand up and leave the room. No sooner would I have passed through the door than I would have slipped into the void.

A bearded man came in with a camera on a shoulder strap, bringing in a breath of cold air from outside. I was suddenly jolted out of my stupor. It was the photographer with his velvet jacket and the face of an art-school student, the one who patrolled the sidewalk in front of the Palais de la Méditerranée and who had taken a picture of the Neals, Sylvia, and me. I kept that photo in my wallet at all times.

He made his rounds from table to table, asking the diners if they wanted a "souvenir photo," but none of them said yes. Then it was my turn. He seemed to hesitate, probably because I was alone.

"Photo?"

"Yes, please."

He raised his camera, and the flash blinded me.

He waited for the picture to dry between his fingers and looked at me with a certain curiosity.

"Alone in Nice?"

"Yes."

"Tourist?"

"Not exactly."

He slipped the photo into a little cardboard frame and handed it to me.

"That'll be fifty francs."

"Would you like to have a drink?" I said.

"Sure."

"I used to be a photographer myself," I said.

"Ah."

He sat across from me and put his camera on the table.

"You took a picture of me once before, on the Promenade des Anglais," I said.

"I don't remember everyone. It's a never-ending parade of people, you know."

"Yes, a never-ending parade."

"So, you used to be a photographer too?"

"Yes."

"What kind?"

"Oh, a little of everything."

It was the first time I had been able to talk to someone. I took the photograph out of my wallet. He glanced distractedly at it, then furrowed his brow.

"Is that one of your friends?" he asked, pointing to Neal.

"Not really."

"Imagine that—I used to know him back in the day. But I haven't seen him for years. I didn't even realize I was taking his picture that day. They all go by so fast . . ."

The waiter brought us two flutes of champagne. I pretended to take a sip, while he emptied the glass in one gulp.

"So, you knew him?" I said, without hoping for much from his answer, since I was used to things slipping away before my eyes.

"Yes. We used to live in the same neighborhood when we were kids. In Riquier."

"You're sure?"

"Positive."

"What was his name?"

He thought I was testing him. "Alessandri. Paul Alessandri. Is that the right answer?"

He didn't take his eyes off the photograph.

"And what is Alessandri up to now?"

"I don't know exactly," I said. "I hardly know him."

"The last time I saw him, he was a bull-herder in the Camargue." He looked up and said, in a tone ironic and solemn at once: "That's some bad company you're keeping, my friend."

"What do you mean?"

"Paul started out as a bellboy at the Ruhl. He worked as a currency exchanger at the city casino, then as a bartender. He went up to Paris and I lost sight of him . . . He did some time in jail . . . If I were you, I'd be careful." He fixed his small, piercing eyes on me. "I always try to warn tourists."

"I'm not a tourist," I said.

"Oh, you live in Nice?"

"No."

"Nice is a dangerous town," he said. "You meet some bad people here . . ."

"I didn't know his name was Alessandri," I said. "He called himself Neal."

"Ah. What was that name you said?"

"Neal." And I spelled it for him.

"Well well, Paul is calling himself Neal? Neal . . . That was an American who lived on Boulevard de Cimiez when we were kids. In a big villa. Château Azur. Paul used to have me over to play in the villa's gardens with him. It was right after the war. His father was the gardener there."

■

I crossed Place Masséna. The police prefecture was a little farther up, past the construction fence around the site of the old municipal casino where Paul Alessandri had been a currency exchanger. What did that mean, "exchanger"? I paced back and forth, looking at the buses entering and leaving the bus station. Then I went through the archway in one swift move, as though I was afraid I might turn back.

I asked the man sitting behind a desk in the lobby which department handled disappearances.

"What kind of disappearance?"

I was already sorry I was here. Now I would be asked all kinds of questions and would have to give detailed answers. Evasive replies wouldn't work. I could already hear the monotonous clicking of the typewriter.

"A missing person," I said.

"Second floor. Room 23."

I wanted to take the stairs instead of the elevator. I went down a light-green hallway lined with odd-numbered doors: 3, 5, 9, 11, 13 . . . Then another corridor forked off perpendicularly to the left. 15, 17, 23. The globes on the ceiling cast a glaring light on the door, making me blink. I knocked several times. A sharp voice told me to come in.

A blond man with glasses, rather young, was resting his elbows on a metal desk, arms crossed. Next to him was a little white wooden table holding a typewriter in a black plastic cover.

He indicated the chair opposite him. I sat down.

"It's about a friend who disappeared a few days ago," I said, and I heard my voice sounding like somebody else's.

"A friend?"

"Yes. We had met two people, who invited us out to a restaurant, and after dinner she disappeared with them in an Opel . . ."

"Your girlfriend?"

I was speaking very fast, as though I expected to be interrupted at any moment and I didn't have a second to spare to explain everything.

"Since then there's been no word. The people we'd met claimed their names were Mr. and Mrs. Neal, living in a villa on Boulevard de Cimiez belonging to the American embassy. Plus they drove a car with diplomatic plates, which is still parked in front of the villa . . ."

He was listening to me with his chin in his hand, and I

couldn't stop talking. I had kept all these things to myself for so long, without any chance to confide in someone.

"Neal wasn't his name and he wasn't an American like he claimed, his name is Paul Alessandri and he's from Nice. I found that out from one of his childhood friends who's a photographer on the Promenade des Anglais and who took a picture of us."

I took the photograph out of my wallet and handed it to him. He took it carefully between his thumb and his finger, like the wing of a dead butterfly, and placed it on his desk without looking at it.

"Paul Alessandri is the third from the left. He was a bellboy at the Hotel Ruhl. He went to jail . . ."

He pushed the photo toward me with the tips of his fingers. He couldn't be bothered with it. And Paul Alessandri, whether he had spent time in jail or not, held no interest for him.

"My girlfriend was wearing a very valuable jewel . . ."

Everything was about to be turned on its head. I only had to give a few more details and a phase of my life would be over, right there in the police prefecture. The moment had come—I was sure of it—when he would take off the black slipcover and move the typewriter onto his desk. He would slip a sheet of paper into it, turn the squeaking roller. Then he would look up at me and say, in a gentle voice: "I'm listening."

But he didn't move, didn't say a thing, his chin still in the palm of his hand.

"My girlfriend was wearing a very valuable diamond," I repeated, in a firmer voice.

He still said nothing.

"This Paul Alessandri, passing for an American, had spotted the diamond my girlfriend was wearing and even offered to buy it . . ."

He had sat up straight and put both hands flat on the table, like someone wanting to bring a conversation to a close.

"This is about a friend of yours?" he said.

"Yes."

"You're not related to her, then?"

"No."

"The name of our department is Family Tracing Services. If I understand you correctly, this individual is not a member of your family."

"That's right."

"In that case . . ."

He spread his arms with ecclesiastical sweetness, in a gesture of powerlessness.

"Besides, I've seen a lot of this kind of disappearance, you know. Usually runaways. How do you know your girlfriend didn't just feel like taking a trip with this couple? That she won't send word before long?"

I still had the strength to mutter: "I read in the paper that a car, an Opel, crashed into a ravine between Menton and Castellar."

He rubbed his hands together with the same ecclesiastical sweetness. "There are any number of Opels on the Riviera that crash into ravines. You're not saying you want to try to track down all the Opels in and around Nice that crash into ravines?"

He stood up, took my arm, and brought me to the door with a firm but courteous grip. He opened the door.

"I'm sorry. There's really nothing we can do for you."

And he showed me the sign on the door. After he closed it, I stood there for a moment, paralyzed, stupefied, under the globe of light in the hall, staring at the blue letters: "Family Tracing Services."

I found myself back in the Jardin Albert I, feeling that now there was no one who could help me. I was angry at the police functionary for his lack of concern. He hadn't for a second tried to help me, hadn't offered me a lifeline or shown the most basic professional curiosity. He had discouraged me when I was just about to tell him everything. Well, too bad for him. It wasn't a routine matter like he thought. It wasn't. It was his own fault he'd missed out on a good chance for a promotion.

Maybe I had explained it badly: it wasn't Sylvia I should have been talking about, it was the Southern Cross. Compared to the long and bloody history of that diamond, what did our lives matter, our poor little personal affairs? Another episode in the life of the stone had been added to the rest, and it wouldn't be the last.

When we first arrived in Nice, I had discovered, in the bookstore on Rue de France where we used to buy our used mysteries, a three-volume work written by a certain B. Balmaine: *Biographical Dictionary of Precious Stones*. This Balmaine, a diamond expert in the Paris Court of Appeals, had inventoried several thousand precious gemstones. Sylvia and I had looked up the Southern Cross.

Balmaine devoted a dozen lines to our diamond. It had been

among the jewels stolen from the Countess du Barry on the night of January 10 to 11, 1791, then sold at auction by Christie's in London on February 19, 1795. Nothing more was known about it until October 1917, when it was once again stolen, from a certain Fanny Robert de Tessancourt, 8 Rue de Saigon, Paris, 16th. The culprit, one Serge de Lenz, was arrested, but Fanny Robert de Tessancourt quickly dropped the charges, saying that Lenz was her close friend.

The stone did not "resurface"—Balmaine's word—until February 1943, when a certain Jean Terrail sold it to one Pagnon, Louis. According to a later police report, the purchase was made in German marks. Then, in May 1944, Louis Pagnon sold the diamond to one de Bellune, Philippe, known as Pacheco, born in Paris on January 22, 1918, to Mario and Eliane Werry de Hults, place of residence unknown.

The Countess du Barry was guillotined in December 1793; Serge de Lenz was murdered in September 1945; Louis Pagnon was shot in December 1944. De Bellune, Philippe, disappeared like the Southern Cross itself until it reappeared on Sylvia's black sweater and then disappeared again. Along with her . . .

But as night fell in Nice, I started to give the functionary credit. He would have been happy to try to trace her if I were a family member. And if he had taken the cover off his typewriter and started questioning me, how could I have told him Sylvia's story and all the recent events in my life, which even to myself seemed too fragmentary and discontinuous to be understood? Besides, I can't say everything. I need to keep some things for myself. I often think about the old movie poster I once saw scraps of on a fence: MEMORIES ARE NOT FOR SALE.

I went back to the Sainte-Anne Pension. There, in the silence of my room, I heard a noise that often came to me while I couldn't sleep: a typewriter. The clattering of the keys, very fast and then gradually farther apart as if the person was typing with two hesitant fingers. And again I had that blond police functionary before me, questioning me in a muffled voice. It was so hard to know how to answer him.

I should have explained everything, from the beginning. But that was just the problem: there was nothing to explain. In the beginning, it was nothing but a matter of atmosphere, scenery . . .

I would have to show him the photographs I'd taken back on the banks of the Marne. Large black and white photos. I'd kept them, with all the contents of Sylvia's bag. That night, in the room in the Sainte-Anne Pension, I had retrieved them from the bottom of the wardrobe, in the cardboard folder on which was written: "Riverside Beaches."

I had not looked at those pictures for a long time. I now scrutinized their tiniest details and let the backgrounds, the scene of where it had all started, enter into me again. One of the pictures, which I hadn't remembered, made my skin crawl with a feeling of fascination and terror made even more stark by the silence and solitude of my room.

It had been taken a few days before I met Sylvia. Outdoor tables at one of the restaurants along the Marne. Sun umbrellas. Pontoons. Weeping willows. I tried to remember: Was it Le Vieux

Clodoche in Chennevières? Le Pavillon Bleu or Le Château des Îles Jochem in La Varenne? I had hidden with my Leica so that I could capture the people and the scene more naturally.

At one of the tables in back, near the pontoon, with no umbrella, two men were sitting side by side. They were having a friendly conversation. One of them was Villecourt. I immediately recognized the other: it was the man who had introduced himself to us as Neal and whose real name was Paul Alessandri. How strange it was to see him there, sitting on the banks of the Marne, as if the worm were in the apple from the beginning.

Yes, that was where I met Sylvia Heureaux, Villecourt's wife, one summer morning: in La Varenne, at Le Beach. I had come to the banks of the Marne to take photographs a few days earlier. A small press had accepted my proposal for a book called *Riverside Beaches.*

I had showed the publisher the book I was taking as my model: a beautiful album of pictures of Monte Carlo from the late thirties, shot by a photographer named W. Vennemann. My book would be in the same format. The same pagination, black and white photos, most of them back-lit. Instead of the shadows of palm trees outlined against the Bay of Monte Carlo, or the dark, shimmering car bodies at night silhouetted against the lights of the Sporting d'Hiver, there would be the diving boards and pontoons of these beaches outside of Paris. But the light would be the same. The publisher hadn't really understood what I meant.

"The idea is that La Varenne and Monte Carlo are the same?" he'd said.

In the end, he signed a contract with me anyway. People always believe in the young.

■

There were not many people at Le Beach in La Varenne that morning. In fact I think she was the only person sunbathing. Children were hurtling down the long slide into the pool, and you could hear their laughs and screams every time they splashed into the bluish water.

I was struck by her beauty and her languid gestures, the way she lit a cigarette or put the glass of orangeade she was sipping through a straw down next to her. And she lay down on the blue and white striped lounge chair so gracefully, eyes hidden behind sunglasses, that I remembered what my publisher had said. Monte Carlo and La Varenne may not have much in common, but I had just seen one thing: this girl. You could easily imagine her in the same indolent position on Monte Carlo beach, whose ambiance W. Vennemann evoked so perfectly in his black and white photographs. She wouldn't have spoiled the scene, she would have added to its charm.

I was walking back and forth with my camera around my neck, trying to find the best angle.

She noticed what I was doing.

"Are you a photographer?"

"Yes."

She had raised her sunglasses and was looking at me with her bright eyes. The children had left the pool. Only the two of us were left.

"You're not too hot?"

"No. Why?"

I had kept my shoes on—which wasn't allowed in the pool area—and was wearing a turtleneck sweater.

"I've had enough sun," she said.

I followed her to the other side of the pool, where a large ivy-covered wall cast a cool shadow. We sat down on white wooden deck chairs, side by side. She had wrapped a white terry-cloth robe around her. She turned toward me.

"What are you photographing here?"

"The scenery." And with a sweep of my arm I encompassed the pool, the diving board, the water slide, the bathing cabins, and the outdoor restaurant down below, its white arbor on orange posts, the blue sky, the ivy-covered wall green and shady behind us . . .

"I wonder if I shouldn't take color photos after all. That would give people a better sense of the atmosphere here."

She laughed. "You think Le Beach has atmosphere?"

"Yes."

She stared hard at me with an ironic smile. "What kind of pictures do you usually take?"

"I'm working on a book I'm going to call *Riverside Beaches*."

"Riverside beaches?"

She furrowed her brow. I was about to give her the explanation that had already mystified my publisher: the parallels with Monte Carlo, and so on. But it wasn't worth it.

"I'm trying to find all the remaining bathing resorts in the outskirts of Paris."

"Have you found a lot?"

She held out a gold cigarette case, which didn't go with her natural and unaffected appearance. Then, to my surprise, she lit my cigarette for me.

"I've already photographed all the beaches of the Oise— L'Isle Adam, Beaumont, Butry-Plage—and the beach resorts along the Seine: Villennes, Élisabethville . . ."

She was clearly curious about these beaches, which were so nearby but which she had never suspected existed. Her bright gaze pierced me.

"But I think this is my favorite," I said. "This has just the atmosphere I'm looking for. I think I'm going to take a lot of pictures of La Varenne and the area around here."

She didn't take her eyes off me, as though she were trying to tell whether I was joking with her. "You really think of La Varenne as a beach resort?"

"A little. Don't you?"

She laughed again. A very light laugh. "So what do you plan to take pictures of in La Varenne?"

"Le Beach, the banks of the Marne, the pontoons . . ."

"Do you live in Paris?"

"Yes, but I'm staying at a hotel here. I need at least two weeks to take good pictures."

She looked at her watch—a man's watch on a large metal chain band that emphasized how slender her wrist was.

"I have to go back home for lunch," she said. "I'm late."

She had forgotten her gold cigarette case. I bent over to pick it up off the ground and held it out to her.

"Oh, right. I can't forget that. It's a present from my husband."

She said this without conviction. Then she went into one of the cabins on the other side of the pool to change. When she came out, she was wearing a flowered sarong and carrying a large beach bag on her shoulder.

"That's a pretty sarong," I said. "I'd love to take a picture of you in it, here, at Le Beach, or on one of the landings on the Marne. It goes well with the scenery."

"Really? But it's more Tahitian, it's a pareo . . ."

Tahitian, exactly. Vennemann, in his book on Monte Carlo, had included several pictures of the deserted beaches of Saint-Tropez in the thirties. A few women in sarongs were lying on the sand, among the bamboo.

"It is a bit Tahitian," I said, "but that's part of its charm, here along the Marne."

"You're saying you want me to be your model?"

"I'd like that very much."

She smiled at me. We left Le Beach and walked down the middle of the La Varenne road parallel to the Marne. There were no cars. No one. Everything was silent and calm in the sunlight, and all the colors were soft: the blue of the sky, the pale green of the poplars and weeping willows. The water of the Marne, usually murky and stagnant, was light that day, reflecting the clouds, trees, and sky.

We passed the Chennevières bridge and were still walking in the middle of the road, bordered by plane trees, called Promenade des Anglais.

A canoe was floating on the Marne: an almost pink orange. She took my arm and pulled me onto the sidewalk next to the water so we could watch it go by.

She pointed to the gate of a villa. "I live here. With my husband."

Even so, I had the courage to ask if we could see each other again.

"I'm at the pool every day between eleven and one," she told me.

Le Beach was as empty as the day before. She was lying in the sun by the white cabins and I was still looking for the proper angle to take my picture from. I wanted to combine the slide, the cabins, the restaurant's arbor, and the banks of the Marne in one picture. But the riverbanks and Le Beach were separated by the main road.

"It's really too bad they didn't build Le Beach right on the river," I said.

She didn't hear me. Maybe she had fallen asleep under her straw hat and sunglasses. I sat down next to her and put my hand on her shoulder.

"Are you asleep?"

"No."

She took off her sunglasses. She looked at me with her bright eyes and smiled. "Well, have you taken your photos of Le Beach?"

"Not yet."

"You work slowly."

She held her glass of orangeade in both hands, the straw between her lips. Then she held out the glass to me. I took a sip.

"I'd like to invite you over to lunch at our house," she said.

"If it wouldn't be too boring for you to meet my husband and mother-in-law . . ."

"That's very nice of you."

"Maybe it'll inspire you, for your photographs."

"Do you live at La Varenne year-round?"

"Yes. Year-round. With my husband and his mother." She suddenly seemed pensive and resigned.

"Your husband works around here?"

"No. My husband doesn't do anything."

"And your mother-in-law?"

"My mother-in-law? She has horses she enters in harness races at Vincennes and Enghien . . . Are you interested in horses?"

"I don't know much about them."

"Me neither. But if you're interested in them for your photographs, my mother-in-law would certainly be happy to bring you to the racetracks."

Horses. I thought about W. Vennemann, whose book included photographs of the start of the Grand Prix de Monaco, and a bird's-eye view of the cars racing alongside the harbor. Now I had found the equivalent of that sporting event here along the Marne: what could evoke the atmosphere of these riverside beaches that I was looking for better than the harness racehorses and sulkies?

■

She had taken my arm on the empty road running alongside the water, but when we got near her gate she let go.

"It really won't be boring for you to come have lunch with us?" she asked.

"Not at all."

"If you get bored you can always say you have work to do."

The sweet, strange look she gave me was touching. I had the feeling that from that point on we would never be apart.

"I told them you were a photographer and that you were doing a book about La Varenne."

She pushed open the gate. We walked across a lawn in front of a large Normand-style villa, half-timbered. We found ourselves in the living room, dark-wood paneling on the walls and filled with armchairs and a settee, upholstered in plaid.

A woman in beach pants came in through one of the French doors and headed toward us with a smooth and supple walk. She was around sixty, tall, with a mane of gray hair.

"My mother-in-law," Sylvia said, "Madame Villecourt."

"Don't call me your mother-in-law. It depresses me."

She had a husky voice and a slight accent from the outskirts of Paris. "So, you're a photographer?"

"Yes."

She sat down on the settee and Sylvia and I in the chairs. A tray of aperitifs was waiting on the coffee table.

A man with a shuffling walk, short like a jockey, came in. With his white jacket and navy blue pants, he might have been a crew member on a yacht team or someone who worked for a sailing club.

"Help yourself to a drink," Madame Villecourt said.

I poured myself a little port. Sylvia and Madame Villecourt each took a whiskey. The man withdrew, shuffling his feet.

"I hear you're taking pictures for a book about La Varenne?" Madame Villecourt said.

"Yes, La Varenne and all the other riverside beaches around Paris."

"La Varenne has changed a lot . . . It's completely dead now. Sylvia told me you were looking for information about La Varenne, for your book."

I glanced at Sylvia, who was looking at me out of the corner of her eye. So this was the pretext she had used to bring me here.

"I came to La Varenne right after I got married. My husband and I lived in this house."

She helped herself to a second glass of whiskey. She had an emerald ring on her middle finger.

"Back then, there were a lot of actors and filmmakers in La Varenne. René Dary, Jimmy Gaillard, Préjean. The Fratellinis lived in Perreux—my husband knew them all. He used to bet on the races in Tremblay, with Jules Berry . . ."

She seemed happy sitting in front of me listing off these names, calling up these memories. What had Sylvia told her? That I was planning to write a history of La Varenne?

"Living here was practical for them, because Joinville Studios was nearby."

I could tell that she was inexhaustible on the subject. Her cheeks were growing red, her eyes shining. Was it the second glass of whiskey she had downed, or the rush of memories?

"I know a very strange story that might interest you."

She smiled at me and her face was suddenly smooth. A glow of youth had come into her eyes and her smile. She must have once been a very pretty woman.

"It's about another movie person my husband knew well. Aimos, Raymond Aimos . . . He lived very near here, in Chennevières. He was supposedly killed during the liberation of Paris, on a barricade, by a stray bullet."

Sylvia was listening and seemed surprised. Clearly she had never heard her mother-in-law talk in this way, nor, perhaps, ever seen her so relaxed and forthcoming with a stranger.

"In fact, it wasn't that way at all. It's a shady story . . . Let me tell you . . ." Then she shrugged her shoulders. "Do *you* believe in stray bullets?"

▪

A dark-haired man around thirty-five, in sky-blue pants and a white shirt, came and sat down on the couch next to Madame Villecourt at the exact moment when she was about to reveal to me the secret of Aimos's death.

"I can see you're deep in conversation. I hope I'm not interrupting." He leaned over toward me and held out his hand. "Frédéric Villecourt. Nice to meet you. I'm Sylvia's husband."

Sylvia opened her mouth to introduce me but I didn't give her time to say my name. I merely said, "Nice to meet you too."

He looked hard at me. Everything about him—a certain ease; a slightly self-satisfied smile; a metallic, authoritative voice—suggested that he knew he was a dark, handsome man. But his charm evaporated quickly, very quickly, in his utterly graceless gestures, entirely in harmony with the large chain bracelet around his wrist.

"Maman is telling you all her old stories. Once she gets started, she never stops."

"This young man is interested in hearing them," Madame Villecourt said. "He's writing a book about La Varenne."

"Well, you can believe whatever Maman says. She's a fountain of knowledge for everything that has to do with La Varenne."

Sylvia looked down, embarrassed. She had put a hand on her knee and was thoughtfully rubbing its back with one finger.

"I hope we're eating soon," Frédéric Villecourt said. "I'm hungry as a dog!"

She glanced nervously at me as if sorry to have dragged me into this house and inflicted the company of this woman and her son on me.

◼

"We'll be eating outside," Madame Villecourt said.

"That is an excellent idea you have there, Maman," he said, using the formal *vous*.

His using *vous* and his affected tone surprised me. They seemed to go with his giant bracelet too.

The man in the white jacket was waiting in the living room doorway.

"Lunch is served, Madame."

"Coming, Julien," Villecourt shouted.

"Did you put up the canopy?" Madame Villecourt asked.

"Yes, Madame."

We crossed the large lawn, Sylvia and I walking slightly behind the others. She gave me a questioning look and seemed afraid I was going to ditch them.

"I'm glad you invited me for lunch," I said to her. "Very glad."

She didn't seem entirely reassured. Maybe she was afraid of her husband's reaction. She was looking at him in a slightly contemptuous way.

"Sylvia told me you're a photographer," Villecourt said, opening the garden gate and holding it for his mother. "I could give you some work, if you want." He smiled broadly. "Me and a friend are putting together some important business, and we'll need some publicity photos and a brochure."

While he spoke like someone wanting to do a subordinate a favor, I couldn't take my eyes off the bracelet hanging from his wrist—if this "important business" of his was along the lines of that bracelet with its big, fat chain links, then it must be something to do with trafficking in American cars.

"He doesn't need you to give him a job," Sylvia said drily.

■

Right on the other side of the street from the house, on the water, Villecourt pushed open a white barrier on which was written: "Villa Frédéric, Private Deck, 14 Promenade des Anglais."

His mother turned toward me: "You'll have a lovely view of the Marne . . . I'm sure you'll want to take pictures."

We went down a few steps dug into the rock, which was so red it looked fake. Then we stepped out onto a large floating deck with a green and white striped canvas canopy. The table was set for four.

"Please, sit here," Madame Villecourt said, indicating the place with a view of the Marne and the opposite shore. She sat to my left and Sylvia and her husband sat at the ends of the table, Sylvia next to me and Frédéric Villecourt next to his mother.

It took two trips from the villa to the deck for the man in the white jacket to bring us plates of crudités and a large cold fish. He was sweating in the heat. Each time, Villecourt said: "Don't get run over crossing the Promenade des Anglais, Julien!" Julien totally ignored this advice as he moved off, shuffling his feet.

I looked around. The canopy blocked the sun, but the light was reflected by the green, stagnant water of the Marne, making it transparent, like the other day, when we were leaving Le Beach. The Chennevières hillside across from us, with the big buhrstone houses at its base, rose up above the trees. Attractive modern houses all along the water. I pictured them occupied by retired brokers from Les Halles.

The Villa Frédéric's deck where we were having lunch pro-
tected from the sun was the biggest and fanciest in sight, by far.
Even the restaurant less than a hundred feet away to the right,
Le Pavillon Bleu, had a landing that seemed downright modest next to this one. It stood in curious contrast with the landscape of the Marne here—willows, stagnant water, riverbanks
for fishermen.

"Do you like the view?" Madame Villecourt asked.

"Very much."

A curious contrast. It felt like we were eating in a slice of
the Riviera transported to the outskirts of Paris, like the medi-
eval castles that California millionaires brought to America stone
by stone. The rock face leading down to the deck reminded me
of one of the rocky inlets near Cassis. The canopy above us had
a Monacan majesty and could easily have appeared in one of
W. Vennemann's pictures. It recalled the Lido of Venice, too.
My impression was only reinforced when I noticed a Chris-Craft
powerboat moored to the deck.

"Is that yours?" I asked Madame Villecourt.

"No, no. It's my son's. This idiot likes to ride it around on the
Marne even though that's not allowed."

"Don't be nasty, Maman."

"Anyway," Sylvia said, "the boat can't go because of the silt
in the river."

"That's not true, Sylvia," Villecourt said.

"It's a real swamp. If you try to water-ski, the skis get caught
in the sludge, it's like molasses, and you're stuck in the middle

of the Marne." She said this sentence in a cutting voice, staring straight at Villecourt.

"Nonsense, Sylvia. You can drive a Chris-Craft or go water-skiing just fine in the Marne."

He was cut to the quick. The Chris-Craft was clearly a very important matter to him. He turned toward me: "She prefers that crummy Le Beach, which is falling apart . . ."

"No it isn't," I said. "Le Beach isn't falling apart, and I think it's very charming."

"Really?" He stared back and forth at Sylvia and me as if trying to catch us plotting.

"Yes, it's completely stupid, that boat," Madame Villecourt said. "You need to get rid of it."

Villecourt didn't answer. He had lit a cigarette. He was sulking.

"So, what riverside beaches have you found in the area?" Madame Villecourt asked me.

The sunlight reflected from the water made her squint; she put on a large pair of dark sunglasses.

"That's what you're looking for, for your photographs, isn't it? Riverside beaches?"

Her lioness face, her dark glasses, the whiskey she was drinking during lunch, all made her look like an American on vacation at Eden Roc. But there was a difference between her and the Riviera accessories all around us: the rock face, the Chris-Craft, the canopied deck. Madame Villecourt was in harmony with the landscape along the Marne; she resembled it. Maybe it was her husky voice?

"That's right, I'm looking for riverside beaches," I said.

"When I was young I went swimming down there, near Chelles. The Gournay-sur-Marne beach. They called it 'Little Deauville.' There was sand, and canvas tents . . ."

So she grew up here?

"But that's not there anymore, Maman," Villecourt said with a shrug.

"Have you gone to see it?" Madame Villecourt asked me, ignoring her son.

"Not yet."

"I'm sure it's still there," Madame Villecourt said.

"I am too," Sylvia said haughtily, keeping her eyes on her husband.

"There's also Berrctrot beach, in Joinville," Madame Villecourt said. She thought for a moment, and started counting on her fingers. "And Duchet, the restaurant at the Saint-Maurice beach. There's the Île-Rouge sandbar in Saint-Maurice too, and Île aux Corbeaux . . ." One by one she tapped the fingers of her right hand with the index finger of her left.

"The hotel and restaurant at the Maisons-Alfort beach . . . The beach at Champigny, on Quai Gallieni . . . The Palm Beach and the Lido in Chennevières . . . I know them all by heart. I was born in the area."

She took off her sunglasses for a moment and looked at me kindly.

"You see, you have a lot on your plate. It's a real Côte d'Azur here."

"But all those places are gone, Maman," Villecourt repeated, with the hostility of someone who isn't being listened to.

"So? A person can dream, can't she?"

This abrupt way of answering her son surprised me.

"That's right, a person can dream," Sylvia repeated in a bright, clear voice, whose slightly drawling intonation went with the banks of the Marne and all the beaches Madame Villecourt had evoked.

■

"You should take a look at that diamond tomorrow, Maman," Villecourt said. "It's truly exceptional. It would be stupid to pass it up. It's called the Southern Cross."

He had his elbows on the table and was trying harder and harder to persuade her. But she, with her eyes hidden behind her sunglasses, stayed stone-faced and seemed to be staring at a fixed point somewhere on the shady green Chennevières hillside.

Sylvia watched me out of the corner of her eye.

"I'll show it to you," Villecourt said. "It has a long pedigree. A unique piece . . ."

This boy with his bracelet and his powerboat stuck in the Marne—was he a diamond dealer or gemstone broker? Having observed him closely, I couldn't believe in these professional capacities.

"'The seller came to see me here, about a week ago,'" Ville-court said. "If we don't move fast the deal will slip through our fingers."

"What would I do with a diamond?" Madame Villecourt said. "I'm no longer the age when I can wear diamonds."

Villecourt laughed. He looked at Sylvia and me as though to make sure he had witnesses.

"But Maman, I'm not talking about wearing it. All we need to do is buy it at a very good price and then sell it for twice as much."

This time, Madame Villecourt did turn to face her son, slowly raising her sunglasses. "That's ridiculous. Buildings and jewels are always sold at a loss. My dear boy, I'm afraid you're not cut out to be a businessman." She had taken on a tone that was affectionate and contemptuous at the same time.

"Sylvia, don't you think Frédéric would do better not to concern himself with precious stones? It's a difficult line of work, you know, my dear . . ."

Villecourt stiffened and had trouble keeping his composure. He even looked away. As for me, I was no longer looking at the bracelet on his wrist but the sparkling powerboat, gone astray in the turgid, dead waters of the Marne due to a mistake of its driver's. I thought to myself that everything he was involved in, every gesture he made, every last action he tried to undertake would inevitably end in a similar mess. And he was Sylvia's husband.

■

I heard footsteps behind me, and a man Villecourt's age appeared on the deck. Medium height, in a beige linen suit and suede shoes, with beady little eyes and a skull as thick as a ram's.

"Maman, this is René Jourdan."

Villecourt introduced him to his mother with a mix of respect and emphasis, as though this René Jourdan, with his suede shoes, bull's head, and empty eyes, was a very important person.

"Who?" Madame Villecourt said without moving a muscle.

"René Jourdan, Maman."

The man held out his hand to Madame Villecourt. "Good afternoon, ma'am." But she didn't shake hands with him. In her dark sunglasses, she was as indifferent to him as a blind person.

So he held out his hand to Sylvia instead, who half-heartedly shook it with a bad-tempered look on her face. Then he nodded a greeting to me.

"René Jourdan," Villecourt said to me. "A friend." He gestured to the empty chair next to mine, and the man took a seat.

"Guess what, René, I was just talking about the diamond. It's a superb piece, don't you think?"

"Superb," the other man said, with a hint of a smile as empty as his gaze.

Villecourt leaned toward his mother. "The man selling the diamond is a friend of René's." He said it like a character reference, or a mention in the Gotha.

"I was just telling my son that I'm no longer of an age to wear diamonds."

"That's too bad, ma'am. I'm sure you'd be thrilled with this diamond. It's a historical piece. We have a whole dossier about it. It's called the Southern Cross."

"Trust me, Maman, if you put up the money, I promise you I can resell it and make double the price."

"My poor Frédéric . . . And where is it from, this diamond? A burglary?"

A sour laugh escaped the bull-headed man. "Not at all, ma'am. An inheritance. My friend is looking to get rid of it because he needs some liquidity. He runs a construction company in Nice. I can give you full references."

"We can show you the stone, Maman . . . You have to see it with your own eyes before you decide."

"All right," Madame Villecourt said in a weary voice. "Show me this Southern Cross."

"Tomorrow, Maman?"

"Tomorrow, yes," she said with a pensive nod.

"You coming, René?" Villecourt said. "We should see how the work is coming along."

He rose to his feet and stood in front of me. "It might interest you . . . I'm currently redoing a little island in the Marne, past Chennevières. The land belongs to my mother. We're building a pool and a nightclub. But Sylvia must have told you about it, since she seems to have no secrets at all from you."

He had suddenly turned hostile. I didn't respond. The thought of his bulging fingers on Sylvia's body was so repellent that I couldn't bear to be touched by them, it might make us come to blows.

He climbed down the ladder from the deck, followed by the man with the suede shoes and bull's head. They sat next to each other in the Chris-Craft, and Villecourt started it, moving nervously. The powerboat quickly disappeared around the Chennevières bend in the river, but the water was too thick for it to leave a wake of foam behind it.

■

Madame Villecourt said nothing for a long moment, then turned to Sylvia: "Darling, go tell him we're ready for coffee?"

"Of course."

Sylvia stood up and, as she walked behind me, furtively squeezed my shoulders with both hands. I was wondering whether she would come back or just leave me alone with her mother-in-law for the rest of the day.

"Maybe we could sit in the sun," Madame Villecourt said.

We moved to the edge of the deck and sat down in two large blue canvas chairs. She didn't say anything, staring fixedly at the water of the Marne from behind her dark sunglasses. What was she thinking about? Children who never give you the satisfaction you hoped for?

"So, your photographs of La Varenne?" she asked me, politely trying to break the silence.

"I'm taking them in black and white," I said.

"That's the right choice," she said, and her categorical tone surprised me. "If you made them all black, that would be even better. Let me tell you something."

She paused for a moment.

"All along the Marne here, these are sad places. Of course they don't look it, in the sun. But when you get to know them . . . They're poison. My husband was killed in a mysterious car accident on the banks of the Marne. My son was born and grew up here and has turned out a hoodlum. As for me, I've grown old alone in this dreary landscape . . ."

She stayed calm as she was confiding all these things to me. If anything, her voice was detached.

"You're not painting too dark a picture of things?" I said.

"Not at all. I can tell that you are a sensitive young man who picks up on the atmosphere of a place, and that you understand what I'm saying. Make your photographs as black as possible."

"I'll try," I said.

"There has always been something foul and black along the banks of the Marne here . . . Do you know whose money built all these villas in La Varenne? It was money the girls made working in the houses. This was where the pimps and madams retired to. I know what I'm talking about . . ."

She abruptly fell silent, and seemed to be thinking about something.

"Bad people have always come here to the banks of the Marne. Especially during the war. I told you about poor Aimos. My husband liked him very much. Aimos lived in Chennevières. He died on the barricades during the liberation of Paris." She kept looking straight ahead, maybe at the Chennevières hillside where this Aimos had lived. "They said he was hit by a stray bullet. It's not true. Someone was settling a score. It was about certain people who used to come to Champigny and La Varenne, during the war. He knew them. He knew things about them. He had heard them talking, in the bars and hotels around here . . ."

■

Sylvia served us coffee. Then Madame Villecourt, seeming sorry to do it, stood up and shook my hand.

"It was very nice to meet you."

She kissed Sylvia on the forehead. "I'm off to my siesta now, darling."

I walked her over to the foot of the stairs cut into the red rock. "Thank you for everything you told me about the Marne," I said.

"If you want more details, come and see me again. But I'm sure you have a good sense of the atmosphere now . . . Take really black photos. Shadowy."

She stressed the syllables, sha-dow-y, with her accent from the area around Paris.

■

"Unusual woman," I said to Sylvia.

We were sitting on the boards of the deck, our feet hanging over the side, and she had put her head on my shoulder.

"Me too? Do you think I'm an unusual woman?" She used the familiar *tu* with me for the first time.

We stayed there on the landing, watching a canoe glide down the middle of the Marne, the same one as the other day. The water, no longer stagnant, flowed in little shudders.

It was this current that carried the canoe, making it so light, giving its impetus to the long, rhythmic movements of the oars, the current whose rushing we could hear beneath the sun.

■

Little by little, without our noticing, the shadows filled my hotel room. She looked at her watch.

"I'll be late for dinner. My mother-in-law and husband must be waiting for me already."

She stood up, turned the pillow over, and pulled back the curtains. "I've lost an earring."

Then she got dressed in front of the closet mirror. She slipped on her green camisole and the red linen skirt that clung to her waist. She sat on the edge of the bed and put on her espadrilles.

"I might be back soon, if they're playing cards. Or else tomorrow morning . . ."

She softly shut the door behind her. I went out onto the balcony and watched her slim silhouette and red skirt in the twilight, moving down the La Varenne quay.

■

I waited for her all day, lying on the bed in my room. The sun coming through the blinds drew blond spots on the walls and on her skin. Downstairs, in front of the hotel, under the three plane trees, the same boules players kept playing late into the night. We heard them talking and shouting. They had hung light bulbs in the trees, which shone through our blinds too, projecting onto the walls in the darkness rays even brighter than the rays of sunlight. Her blue eyes. Her red dress. Her brown hair. Later, much later, the bright colors faded and I no longer saw anything except in black and white—just as Madame Villecourt had said.

Sometimes she could stay until morning. Her husband had gone on a business trip with the man with the suede shoes, bull's head, and empty eyes, and with the man's friend, the one trying to sell the diamond. She didn't know him, but his name often came up when her husband and Jourdan were talking. His name was Paul.

One night, I woke up with a start. Someone was turning the door handle. I never locked my room, in case Sylvia could get away for a moment and come to me. She walked in. I fumbled for the light.

"No, don't turn it on."

At first I thought she was holding out her hand to shield her eyes from the light of the bedside lamp. But she was trying to hide her face from me. Her hair was disheveled and there was a bleeding cut across her cheek.

"My husband . . ."

She dropped onto the edge of the bed. I didn't have a tissue to wipe the drops of blood off her cheek. "I had a fight with my husband."

She had lain down next to me. Villecourt's bulging fingers, his fat little hand, had struck her face . . . The thought of it made me feel like I was going to throw up.

"That's the last time I'm going to argue with him. We're leaving."

"Leaving?"

"Yes. You and me. I have a car downstairs."

"But where will we go?"

"Look. I took the diamond."

She slipped her hand under her shirt and showed me the diamond, on a delicate chain around her neck.

"We won't have money problems with this."

She took the chain off her neck and slipped it into my hand. "Here, you keep it."

I put it on the nightstand. The diamond scared me as much as the gash on her cheek.

"It's ours now," Sylvia said.

"You really think we should take it?"

She didn't seem to hear me.

"Jourdan and the other guy will demand what my husband owes them. They won't let him go until he gives them back the diamond . . ."

She was talking softly, as though someone might be listening at the door.

"And he'll never be able to give it back. They'll make him pay . . . That's what you get for keeping bad company."

She had brought her face right up to mine and spoken the last sentence into my ear. Then she looked me straight in the eye.

"And I'll be a widow."

A nervous laugh shook us. Then she moved even closer to me and turned off the bedside lamp.

■

The car was parked in front of the hotel under the plane trees, where the men had been playing their interminable game of pétanque. But they were gone, and they had turned off the electric lights in the trees. She wanted to drive. She sat behind the wheel and I got in next to her. A bag was sitting diagonally on the back seat.

We went down Quai de La Varenne one last time, and in my memory the car was driving slowly. I caught sight of the poplars on the small island in the middle of the Marne—saw the island's tall grass, the gymnastics bars, the swing, the island we used to swim out to, a long time ago, before the water was poisoned. On the opposite shore, the dark mass of the Chennevières hillside. One last time, the buhrstone pavilions slipped past, the half-timbered villas, the chalets, the bungalows, built at the turn of the century with the money from the girls . . . The lawns where someone had planted a linden tree. The large boathouse of the Cercle des Sports de la Marne. The Château des Îles Jochem's gate and park.

One last time, before she turned right, Le Beach of La Varenne, where it all started—the waterslide, the changing cabins, the arbor in the moonlight, this place that had seemed so fairy-tale in our childhood summers and which, that night, was silent and empty forever.

That was the moment in our lives when we started to feel anxious, a diffuse sense of guilt and the certainty that we had to run away from something, without knowing exactly what. This flight would take us to many different places before finally bringing us here, to Nice.

When Sylvia was lying next to me I couldn't resist taking the diamond in my fingers, or watching it sparkle on her skin, and thinking that it would bring us bad luck. But I was wrong. Others before us had fought for it, others to come would wear it around their neck for a time, or on their finger, and it would traverse the centuries, hard and indifferent to the passing of time and the deaths of those it would leave behind. No, our anxiety didn't come from our contact with that cold stone with glints of blue—it doubtless came from life itself.

Still, at first, when we'd just left La Varenne behind, we knew a brief period of calm and peace. At La Baule in Brittany, in August. We'd rented a room next to a miniature golf course, from an agency on Avenue des Lilas. The shouting and laughter of the minigolf players, which went on until almost midnight, lulled us to sleep. We could have a glass of wine without attracting anyone's notice at one of the tables under the pine trees in front of the kiosk with the green slate roof where they handed out the golf clubs and white balls.

It was very hot that summer, and we were sure no one would find us there. In the afternoons we would walk along the embankment to the most crowded part of the beach. Then we would walk down to the sand, looking for a tiny place free where we could lie on our beach towels. We were never as happy as we were then, lost in a crowd smelling of tanning oil. Children were building sandcastles all around us and the ice cream vendors walked by offering their wares, stepping over the bodies on the sand. We were like everyone else, there was nothing to set us apart from the others, those Sundays in August.

PATRICK MODIANO, winner of the 2014 Nobel Prize in Literature, was born in Boulogne-Billancourt, France, in 1945, and was educated in Annecy and Paris. He published his first novel, *La Place de l'Etoile*, in 1968. In 1978, he was awarded the Prix Goncourt for *Rue des Boutiques Obscures* (published in English as *Missing Person*), and in 1996 he received the Grand Prix National des Lettres for his body of work. Mr. Modiano's other writings include a book-length interview with the writer Emmanuel Berl and, with Louis Malle, the screenplay for *Lacombe Lucien*.

DAMION SEARLS has translated thirty books, including Patrick Modiano's *Young Once*, and is the author of essays, poems, a book of short stories, and *The Inkblots*, a history of the Rorschach test and the first biography of its creator, Hermann Rorschach.